SECRETS AT THE CAFÉ

A NOVEL OF SUSPENSE ABOUT FAMILY AND
FRIENDSHIP

FAMILY SECRETS SERIES

SUSAN SPECHT ORAM

SOS COMMUNICATIONS

SECRETS AT THE CAFÉ

A Novel of Suspense about Family and Friendship

SUSAN SPECHT ORAM

SOS Communications LLC

Published by SOS Communications LLC in 2023

www.susanspechtoram.com

First Edition

ISBN: 979-8-9870410-9-3 (paperback)

ISBN: 979-8-9891982-0-7 (e-book)

❦ Created with Vellum

HER LAST REQUEST

Holding my grandmother's cold hand, I consider her request. Tears trickle down my cheeks, and I wipe them away. Gigi wants me to return home and run her restaurant in the old house where she raised me.

I swallow hard. I want to please her, but saying yes will change my life forever. I will have to leave the life I carved out as an artist in the city. I never pictured myself moving back to my small home town.

Gigi wheezes with each labored breath.

The hospice nurse, who left an hour ago, said my grandmother probably wouldn't make it through the night. My aunt and my cousin were called away. I'm alone with Gigi as she walks her last mile.

The air in the second-floor bedroom is stale. A tree branch skitters against the window glass. I stand up and slide the window open. A gentle breeze blows in.

Resting my hands on my hips, I stare out into the dark night. My grandmother did so much for me when I was growing up. Now I have a chance to return the gift and give her an answer that will offer her peace at the end.

She moans.

I pat her thin shoulder and say in a choked voice, "Of course, I will run the café. Your restaurant will welcome guests forever."

She says in a faint voice, "Find my journal. Read it."

I raise my eyebrows. I didn't know she kept a journal. Scanning the room, I don't see a diary. I'll have to search the two-story house to find it.

"I will," I say. "I love you. Don't worry. I'll run Gigi's for you."

I tiptoe into the bathroom and close the door. In the pink-tiled room, I sob as quietly as I can, sucking in great gulps of air. Her request has upended my life, changing it forever.

1
---

igi's Café is hopping. Locals and tourists occupy every seat. I carry a fresh pot of coffee and pause to sniff the air. Gigi passed away a month ago, but her lavender scent lingers in the old two-story house near downtown.

After she died, I closed for a day and posted a sign saying, "Death in the family. Will re-open tomorrow." Gigi would have wanted me to serve her loyal customers and not wallow in grief.

A couple sits at a two-top reading the local paper. Bets and Zerk are regulars, and they bartend at my favorite pub.

I say, "Hey, you two. More coffee?"

"You bet," Zerk says, wiggling a finger in his ear. "And a gallon more where that came from."

I pour hot black coffee into two mugs and can't help but overhear their conversation.

Bets taps the paper, open to the obituaries, and says to her husband, "This says to share condolences at the family's home."

I glance over her shoulder. The notice is for someone my grandmother knew.

Zerk nods. "A crook could blend in and case the joint, going back when no one's home."

As I turn to the next table, Bets says, "It's tempting, but we won't bite."

Zerk's voice cuts through the din in the room. "Nope, we left our life of crime behind."

My eyebrows shoot up. I didn't know about their hidden past. I'll have to keep a closer eye on cash in the till. But no one will steal from Gigi's. The cash register is in full view of everyone. My grandmother never worried. She trusted people.

A customer asks for water, and I hurry into the kitchen. Leaning against the sink, I let out a breath. My feet throb. My arches ache. I had no idea what I was getting into when I agreed to take over Gigi's Café. I'm in a marathon, starting over every day.

Bob Brinker and his children are finishing their meal in the dining room, which is usually off-limits to customers. He's wearing a gold watch, and his silver hair is trimmed above the collar. They live in a gated community up in the hills. I remember him and his kids, who are about my age, from when I was in high school.

I refill their water glasses. My brow furrows when I notice a built-in drawer in the wall is ajar. I haven't found time to organize Gigi's private papers or sort through her things. I must find the journal she wanted me to read.

Mr. Brinker says, "More ice please."

I say, "Right away."

Ellie Robinson calls from the parlor, "We need glasses for our champagne." She's in a black sweater and yoga pants. Her dark brown shoulder length hair has red high-lights to match her nail polish. She runs her law practice from home while raising their young daughter, Maddie, who is scribbling on a notepad.

"I'll be right back with them," I say.

To her daughter, I say, "I like your blue dress."

Maddie looks up and gives me a smile. Her father, Kenny Robinson, owns the local sporting goods store. He tugs on a sport coat worn over a yellow polo shirt. His oldest daughter, Wanda, is in a paisley dress that's riding up on her thighs.

Ellie says, "Karina, you're terribly busy this afternoon. Is anyone helping you?"

My pulse pounds. Laughter fills my grandmother's two-story home, which I have inherited. Customers are waiting for slices of quiche and scones. The orders are a tsunami of demands. Throwing bowls on a potter's wheel in the city was peaceful compared to serving food.

"My cousin Lydia was supposed to be helping me," I say, glancing around. "But I haven't seen her in about half an hour. Maybe she took a break and didn't tell me."

"This is a lot to take on by yourself, after just moving back."

I sigh. "I thought I knew it all after helping Gigi for so many years. But it's a bigger challenge than I realized."

Striding to the kitchen, I open the freezer and find a single ice cube left in a tray. Thanks a lot, Lydia. My cousin left a glass filled with ice cubes, so I pull that out and refill the trays with water.

I wipe sweat from my upper lip and open the kitchen cupboard doors, looking for glasses for the Robinsons. My jaw drops open. The shelves are bare. All the glasses are out with the guests, which is how my grandmother referred to her customers.

My hands tremble. I am failing at the task she wanted me to take over. Gigi would have handled a Friday afternoon record-breaking rush like this with ease and grace.

I set a glass with ice cubes in front of Brinker, who runs a software company based in town. "I apologize, but this is all the ice we have for now. I'm making more."

"You're swamped," Boots, his daughter, says. She flicks back her long black hair. "But this'll do, thanks."

She's a few years younger than me and is in college. I have changed since I lived here before. I now color my hair pink and wear a tiny diamond stud in my nose.

When Gigi saw what I looked like when I came home,

she burst into tears. "You were perfect, the way you were." She washed scone dough off her hands and gave me a huge hug. "And I love you just the same."

Needing drinking containers for the Robinsons, who are waiting in the parlor, I rummage through the dining room cupboards for champagne glasses. I take two shot glasses, a small pitcher, and a bud vase into the kitchen to wash them.

As the water runs, I swallow. My throat is dry, but I don't have time to stop and quench my thirst. My grandmother would not be pleased with how I'm running her business. Not at all.

But I'm doing the best I can with the questionable help I'm getting from my younger cousin. I bet she took off to see her new boyfriend, who I haven't met yet.

I carry the odd assortment of drinking vessels to the parlor. "I'm sorry, but this is all I have left to drink from. I didn't expect this many people on a Friday afternoon."

Wanda Robinson reaches for the small pitcher. "I'll use this one. What an unusual celebration this is turning out to be, isn't it?"

Mr. Robinson pops the cork and pours champagne. He raises his vase. "A toast to Wanda, for completing her MFA. I knew you could do it."

"MFA," her younger sister, Maddie says, banging her fork on the table. "MFA."

My armpits are damp with sweat. I scurry around the café serving scones and quiche, and topping off cups of coffee. How did my grandmother do this for so many years? Gigi never complained.

By the time I enter the dining room to check on the Brinkers, I'm out of breath.

Boots holds up a red leather notebook. "I found this while we were waiting. I got bored and looked around. It was in a drawer over there."

My eyes grow wide. She opened a drawer below the mirror in the dining room? But her prying is my fault. I was overwhelmed with the overflow crowd and seated them in a private area of the house. I tried to turn Brinker away and told him to come back another day, but he slipped me a ten-dollar bill.

Brinker said, "We were counting on eating your delicious scones, and we're hungry. Couldn't you squeeze us in somewhere?"

Boots said, "Anywhere will be fine. We don't mind. Is the dining room open? Your grandmother let us sit there when all the other seats were taken."

I tucked the money into my apron pocket, wiped my hands on my leather pants and led them to the dining room table.

"Right this way," I said.

Now, I study the red leather diary. I haven't had the courage to comb through Gigi's things. This must be the journal she mentioned. I smile, thinking of how I'll examine it after I close the café for the day.

My fingertips tingle. I reach out for the diary. "I'll take it."

Boots opens the book and points to a page. She says, "There's an interesting part right here. The writer mentions a stock market crash and withdrawing money from the bank. They make it sound like the money is hidden somewhere."

A murmur goes around the table.

Guns, her brother, holds out a hand. "Let me see it."

Boots holds it away from him. "I found it, and I'm not finished with it."

I glance over her shoulder at my grandmother's cursive writing and read: "Monday, October 19, 1987. Stock market crashed. Emptied my bank account and put it somewhere safe."

Blood whooshes in my ears. My grandmother never showed me her diary. She didn't mention hiding money. We could have used that when I was growing up. It might have put me through college.

"I'll take that," I say.

But before I can grab it, a customer taps me on the shoulder.

"I'd like to pay," she says, tugging on a strand of long blond hair. "My son spilled hot chocolate all over. It's dripping on the carpet. I'm sorry, but we're in a hurry. We have to leave right now."

I turn to Boots, who is reading the journal. It would be rude to wrest it out of her hands. I don't want word getting around town that I'm a poor substitute for my grand-mother. I say, "Please give me the notebook."

She shakes her head. "I just want to read one more page."

The woman taps me on the shoulder. "Can you ring us up? We've got to go."

I say to Boots, "I've got to help this guest. Please leave the diary on the table when you go."

Brinker says, "Pass it over, I'd like to take a look at it."

"Me too," Guns says.

Mopping up warm spilled cocoa, I wonder if it's true Gigi withdrew money from the bank. If so, did she put it back? I don't think she would hide it. But she did like trea-sure hunts when I was young.

Guests line up to pay. By the time I get a chance to go into the dining room, the Brinkers have left. Mr. Brinker put a fifty-dollar bill under a water glass on the table.

I shove the money into the pocket of my grandmoth-er's flowered apron. The red journal is not on the table. Perhaps Boots put the notebook back where she found it.

I yank open the drawer and paw through the contents. But I don't find the diary. With trembling hands, I open the other drawers and riffle through papers.

I turn to the table, picking up napkins and peering under plates. I scan the room. There's no sign of the red leather journal.

My heart thumps. Gigi's journal is missing. Her secrets

and private thoughts will be spread all over town if I don't find it.

When I packed up in Seattle and rushed home to Millersville because my grandmother was ill, Gigi held my hand and said, "There is more hidden in this house than you realize. After I'm gone, look for clues."

I put a hand to my forehead and groan. "What have I done?"

Just then, my younger cousin Lydia breezes in through the front door.

"I had an errand to run. How's it going?"

My aunt doesn't like Lydia's new boyfriend, so Lydia has been sneaking around seeing him when she's scheduled to work for me. I hear he's my age, twenty-four years old, and I share my aunt's concern. Lydia just turned eighteen, and she is beautiful. Her skin glows, and her hair shines.

"Don't slack off," I say, "if you want to get paid by me and have money to attend community college."

She flops in a chair. "I can't help it. I'm in love. You wouldn't understand."

"Come on, we've got a lot of work to do."

I head into the kitchen and a flicker of a frown crosses my face.

I understand way more than she knows.

2

L ater that day, the tables are cleared, the floors are swept, and the dishwasher is running. My cousin and I are washing the pots and pans. My grandmother's business offers quiche and scones. If you want a salad, you'll have to go elsewhere. People say they like the limited menu. They know what they'll get, and they can bring their own bottles of alcohol for a corkage fee.

Gigi said, "I'm not expanding the menu. Those skinny women can get salads somewhere else. I want hungry people who appreciate good, home-cooked food."

Gigi's idea turned out to be a success, and one she gifted to me in her will, along with the house. My aunt was deeded her residence, a block down the street, that Gigi bought. Aunt Jean didn't want the big house with moss on the roof. She runs a business doing clothes alterations out of her place. When she welcomed me back to town, she asked me to hire Lydia.

"Keep her busy," my aunt said. "She has too much time on her hands."

And that's what I've been trying to do.

Lydia hands me a pan dripping with water.

I give it back. "You missed a spot, right there."

"Whatever."

As she scrubs, I say, "Remember the family in the dining room?"

"Yeah." She turns to me and smiles. "Bob Brinker and his kids Boots and Guns."

Cocking my head, I say, "Who would call their kids by those names? I don't understand it."

"They were hassled about it at school, and now they act like they have something to prove, like they're better than everyone else."

"Where could I find Boots?"

"She's in college in Bellingham."

"Do you have her cell number? I need to text her and ask something."

Lydia hands me a quiche pan to dry. "Why? What's going on? You look upset."

I say, "When they were at the dining table, Boots opened a drawer and found a journal. It was Gigi's. Boots was supposed to leave it on the table, but it's gone. She must have taken it with her."

Lydia shrugs. "Maybe Boots left it, but someone else took it. What does it look like? Maybe I've seen it around."

I study the ceiling, trying to remember. "It's small, maybe four by six inches, with a red leather cover."

Lydia frowns. "People shouldn't go through Grandma's things. They should know better than to snoop. It's your house. If I see Boots, I'll tell her you want to talk to her."

"It might be best not to mention the diary, in case she took it on purpose. I want to surprise her."

I think back to Wanda Robinson, who has a master's degree in creative writing. If I was a writer, I might use Gigi's journal as a springboard for a novel.

"What about the Robinsons?" I say. "Do you know them?"

Lydia shakes her head and turns off the tap. She wipes her hands on a towel.

"Not really. Got to run."

"Come back tomorrow morning," I say, "and help me make quiches."

But she's already out the door.

3

The next day, I pull on jeans and a shirt at five in the morning. The wood floor boards are cool under my bare feet. Throwing a robe on over my clothes for warmth, I pull up the window blinds. It's dark outside. No cars are driving by. Dog walkers are not out yet. It's too early for anyone else to be up.

I yawn and shuffle downstairs, heading into the kitchen. I splash cold water on my face to wake up before brewing a pot of coffee. Then I get serious about baking.

At six o'clock, I unlock the front door in case Lydia stops by to help.

I'm opening the oven when a noise makes me jump in the air.

My heart races. The front door slams. Windows rattle.

I call out, "Lydia, is that you?"

If it's her, she'd be early, which would be a first.

Floorboards creak with each foot step.

I grab the rolling pin and go to face whoever is invading my home.

"Lydia's missing," my aunt says, with a frantic look on her face. "Is she here?"

Her face is flushed, and she's breathing hard. She must have run here from her house. She darts into the parlor, the dining room, and the café. She opens the closet doors and checks under tables.

"What's going on?" I say, resting a hand on her shoulder.

She blows out a breath, and her bangs flutter like feathers in the wind.

"We had a fight over the man she's seeing, and I said some things I regret. I think she ran off with him."

I nod. I understand about impulsive young love which is thwarted by a guardian. It happened to me in high school. But these days, I'm solo and keeping to myself when I'm not working.

"If she ran off, she'll reach out to me," I say. "I'll tell her you're looking for her."

My aunt opens the front door. "If she calls or texts you, please let me know."

"I will. If I didn't have to open in an hour, I'd help you look."

She turns. "And tell her I love her, will you?"

She closes the door with a thwack. The windows vibrate.

As an excuse to check on my cousin, I text her to see if she's coming into work to help me cook.

"Be right there," she texts back.

As I slide a pan of scones into the hot oven, Lydia comes in.

She throws her denim jacket over a chair. "Here I am, right on time."

I give her a hug, and she wraps her arms around me, holding me tight.

"I miss Gigi," she says.

I let out a sigh. "I miss her like rain in August, when you wonder if moisture will ever fall. We're in a dry spell without Gigi's smile. It's going to take a while to adjust."

She pulls away. "I don't get what you said, but I think I know what you mean."

I say to the house and the woodwork she polished with Lemon Pledge, "We miss you, Gigi."

"We do," Lydia says, looking up. Turning to me, she says, "What do you need me to do?"

"I've got scones in the oven. We need to make quiches."

She rolls her eyes. "The crusts. It's always the crusts. The crusts are a pain to make."

"I agree. But let's get going. We open in an hour."

While we roll out dough, the smell of baking scones

fills the kitchen. My stomach growls. I take a tray of scones from the oven and grab a Tillamook Oregon Strawberry yogurt from the frig.

"Want one?"

Lydia shakes her head. "I'm set."

I lean against the counter, eating yogurt. "You and your mom had a fight?"

She bears down on the rolling pin.

"I told her I might move in with my boyfriend. She's blowing it out of proportion."

The spoon falls out of my hand, clattering on the counter. Drops of pink yogurt splatter. I grab a sponge and wipe up the mess.

"You're just eighteen. Can you even do that? And what about the age difference between you?"

She plops a crust into a pie pan, smooths it out, and crimps the edges.

"I don't care. I just want to be with him. We were going to move in together after I finish high school, but why wait that long?"

I nod. Life is too short to wait. I know that all too well, because today is the anniversary of the day my parents died. I fiddle with my earlobes. My earrings are missing. I touch my nose. I forgot to put in my diamond post. Normally I put product in my hair each morning, but I neglected to do that today.

"Today is the day my parents died. When the other driver tied her shoes," I say in a soft voice, "while going down the road. She hit my parents head on. At least, that's what I was told."

I wipe away tears. I've heard different versions of how my folks died. In one, the car hit a tree. Or, the brakes failed. Or, a woman was at fault. Was Gigi protecting me from the truth?

Lydia sighs. "I forgot it was today. I'll make it up to you and work extra hard."

Sliding quiche crusts in the oven to pre-bake, I turn on the mixer and whip eggs in a stainless mixing bowl. Beater blades chatter against the sides of the metal bowl.

Turning off the mixer, I say, "Your mom's worried about you. And I am too."

"I'm fed up with people telling me I'm too young," she says. "And who's my mom to tell me that? She's a hypocrite. She was wild when she was my age. I've heard stories."

Pulling out piping hot crusts, I pour in filling and tuck the quiches into the oven. Lydia's right. When I was in high school, Gigi told me stories about raising Aunt Jean and my mother. She said I had to be better behaved, and she was through with trying to tame rebellious teenage girls.

Lydia says, "I saw Boots by the way. Last night at Dirty J's."

"Did you get her cell number?"

She shakes her head. "She was dancing with a guy

named Colt. The music was too loud to talk. But she'll be at her dad's all week."

Drumming my fingers on the counter, I hang on every word. I must find Gigi's journal. "After we close, I'll head out to see Boots at her house."

"I'll go with you, and we'll give my name to the guard. You can just come along. That way they won't have a heads up you're coming and hide the journal before we arrive. But you'll have to do something for me in exchange."

This kid cousin has nerve, and I admire her for it. I tilt my head. "And what might that be?"

"My mom comes in the basement when we're on the couch down there, and she does loads of laundry when my boyfriend is over. If we're in my room, she knocks and tells me to leave the door open. She won't let me go over to his place. We need to hang out here instead."

If I were Lydia's mother, I'd keep eyes on her from various viewpoints in the house too, finding excuses to pop in and check. But it would help if Lydia was with me when I spoke with Boots about the diary. I'm feeling nervous about going by myself.

"Fine," I say, "if you go with me to see Boots, you can hang out with your boyfriend at my place for one evening. And he has to leave by ten."

She flashes a white smile. "Five nights, and he leaves at midnight."

"Two nights, and you're out by ten at the latest. That's my final offer."

She taps a toe.

The timer dings.

The quiches are ready.

"Fine," she says, "but let me do the talking at their house. I know them, and you don't. I have a reputation to protect."

4

My calves ache from being on my feet and moving at a fast clip as I serve customers. People smile and eat warm scones. They scarf down slices of bacon-cheddar quiche. Only crumbs remain on white plates when I clear vacated tables. Hearing thanks from happy diners fueled Gigi, giving her endless energy. I am beginning to understand why she loved her career. It is satisfying to serve a meal and receive praise.

The crowd thins out, and a few tables are empty. A woman in her thirties enters the café, looking around. Violet is fit, and she is ex-military. She started her own security services firm and saved our town from disaster the other week when peaceful protests bloomed into all out riots. A reporter told us we look alike, with the same bump on our noses, but I don't see the resemblance. But we are both small business owners and members of the Chamber of Commerce.

I point to a table. "That one's open. I'll get your coffee and water."

I hurry off to bring her beverages. Violet is a runner. When she comes in, she asks for water and likes to stay hydrated.

I set a steaming hot cup and a glass of cold water in front of her.

Violet says, "We still need to grab that beer at the Brown sometime. My schedule is open, now that the dust has settled down in town." She wipes her brow. "That was some week we had, wasn't it?"

I glance around the room, making sure no one needs my immediate attention, and then sink into the seat opposite her. "I couldn't believe your mother was in the thick of it, on opposite sides of the struggle. Did your relationship with her survive the riots, I hope?"

She doesn't answer for a beat. She comes in often, and we have chatted before, so I feel comfortable asking her questions like this and exchanging personal information.

I say, "The reason I ask is my mom died when I was young. My grandmother raised me, but she's gone. I guess I'm a little jealous that you can call your mother when you want. I don't have anyone."

Lydia bustles by, refilling coffees. She says to me, "Don't forget, we're just down the street. You are not alone." She moves on to serve other tables.

Violet taps a trimmed fingernail on the table. "I'm sorry to hear that. It must be rough."

I nod and bite my lower lip.

Violet says, "About my mom and the protests in town, I've been trying to let it go. But a bunch of them broke into my house not once, but twice, and it was my mother's idea."

My mouth drops open. "Your own mother broke into your place?"

Violet frowns. "They trashed the place, broke a table, and had a bonfire on my new patio. It took three of us to boot them out the last time. So, it's going to take me a while to get over what happened." She rubs her forehead. "But she raised me, and I love her deep down. We're trading texts and emails for now."

A concerned look crosses her face. I wonder if something else is bothering her, something she doesn't want to discuss it with me. We have a lot in common, but we're not close friends.

I stand and say, "What'll you have? The usual? Just a scone?"

She gives me a smile. "I ran ten miles this morning, so I'll have a scone and a slice of your quiche. It smells delicious."

I head into the kitchen to fill her order and sigh. I miss Gigi and my parents more than ever. Reading my grandmother's diary will comfort me, I imagine, when I can get my hands on it. I make a vow to recover Gigi's journal.

With Lydia's help, I'll follow the trail after work and track it down this afternoon.

I wipe tears from my eyes and carry on, just like my grandmother would have wanted.

At three o'clock, I box up a to-go order for a man in his seventies wearing a black fedora. His red lapel button catches my eye, bringing my mind back to the red diary. I want it back in my hands and under my roof, where it belongs. I should never have left it out of my sight.

Finally, at four o'clock, I turn the Open sign on the front door to Closed.

Lydia is at the kitchen sink, scrubbing pots.

"Leave the dishes," I say to her. "I'll do them later. Let's head over to Field Estates. I want to talk to Boots and get Gigi's journal from her. And I swear, that's the last time I'll seat people in a private part of the house, even if they bribe me to fit them in."

She says, "But we can't turn customers away. You need the money."

Her head turns to the back door.

A tall man stands there. He is back lit, and I can't get a good look at him.

"You're here," she says, waving him over with a wide smile. "Come meet my cousin."

She says to me, "I told him he could come with us. He's studying architecture and wants to see what the houses look like in Field Estates."

I make a face, because I was looking forward to time

alone with my cousin. Being her boss is a natural set-up for friction between us, especially given how she's been ignoring her job and flitting out the door to see her boyfriend.

He steps forward, and I get a good look at him. My eyes grow wide.

"Karina," Lydia says, "this is Shane."

He holds out his hand. We shake, and his grip is firm.

"Nice to see you again," he says. He has grown a beard since I last saw him.

I let out a chuckle, but it sounds more like the cry of a strangled seagull. I can't believe my former high school boyfriend is dating my younger cousin. "How many years has it been?"

"Too long." He wipes his hands on his jeans.

Mine are moist, and I mimic his gesture.

"You two know each other?" Lydia says. She looks at me and then at Shane.

Shane and I nod, locking eyes. His brown eyes draw me in, like in the old days.

Lydia says, "How?"

"We were in preschool through part of high school together," he says.

Shane gave me my first kiss at age six. A kiss on the cheek, to be sure, but he was the one. We went out in high school. But then he moved out of town.

"You came back to attend college?" I say.

"Yep, how about you?"

I rub my cheek. Everything about this scene is wrong. He should know better than to date my younger cousin. She is in high school. He should be going out with someone closer to our age.

I shove my hands in my pockets. "Gigi asked me to come home and run the cafe, and I wanted to make her happy. So here I am." I shrug to cover my discomfort.

He smiles and pushes the hair out of his eyes. "Not me, I'm off to Europe after this to see the world's most beautiful buildings."

Lydia tugs on his arm. "You didn't tell me that."

He cocks his head. "We've been doing other things, with not much talking."

I squint at him to communicate he's dating someone way too young for him. He smiles, so I don't think he got my message. If I get him alone, I'll mention it, but not in front of Lydia. She would be angry at me for interfering in her private life.

But I am family, and I know what is best for her. Besides, my aunt would want me to talk some sense into Shane, if she realized I knew him. Their age difference bothers her.

He says, "Something in your eye?"

I blink. "I'm fine."

"Ready to go?" he says. "Or should we clean up the kitchen first?"

Lydia places her hand in Shane's, interlocking fingers. She stares at me like I'm a threat and competing for his attention. "Let's go. She wants to find my grandmother's journal."

"That's right." I say, locking up the house and leading them to my car. "Thanks for the offer to wash dishes. You may regret that."

"No big deal," he says. "Anytime, for an old friend. We can talk about what we've been up to since we saw each other last."

Lydia shoots him a sharp look.

He gets in the back, and Lydia slides in next to him. Alone in the front seat, I guess they expect me to be their chauffeur. I am an outsider, a feeling that has haunted me since my parents died. I am the only one in the car who isn't in love.

Shane says to Lydia, "It's rude to ride in the back while she drives. Sit with your cousin. I'll be fine on my own."

I've been on my own since moving back home to Millersville. I left my life as an artist in the city, where I sold my wares at street fairs and in galleries. Selling pottery and paintings wasn't the most lucrative of careers, but I was in my element and doing what I loved. Creativity mattered more to me than fancy clothes or dinners out.

Lydia groans. She climbs out and flops in the front passenger seat. She crosses her arms.

I suppress a smile. When I was her age, every feeling was amplified. Now, after having been with Gigi on the day of her death, everything has come into focus. What matters most is family and letting them know I love them.

When I check the rearview mirror, Shane winks at me.

I wish I didn't agree to let them hang out at my house for two evenings. Nothing is worse than a couple necking in close proximity. The sound of smacking lips will carry through the thin-walled building. I'll have to muffle it and wear headphones, listening to music.

I drive to Field Estates and grip the wheel tight. Knowing Shane makes an awkward situation much worse. If I happen to walk by and see them in a passionate embrace, I'll have to separate them like my aunt Jean definitely would. I'm not looking forward to spending several cringe-worthy evenings with them and can't wait to get my obligation over with.

I glance over at Lydia. She wants the freedom that comes with being an adult. But from her tight jeans and low-cut crop tops, I think she needs a little oversight.

Lydia reaches back to hold his hand, and I crank up the radio, humming along.

Shane says, "If the diary was in your house in the first place, why does someone else have it?"

I explain what happened yesterday afternoon and say, "But Boots might not have it. I'm not sure where it is or who took it."

He nods. "I hope you find it."

Lydia clamps a hand on my arm. "We'll help you find the journal, if Boots doesn't have it." She turns to the backseat. "Won't that be fun?"

A groan escapes my lips. I'm better off doing things

alone. I don't need their help. The greater the distance between her boyfriend, who stole my heart and never called after he moved, and me, the better.

I tap the steering wheel. "Maybe. We'll see."

Lydia pouts. "That's what my mom says when she means no."

"I'm not sure of anything yet."

Upheaval has been my middle name these past few months. I left a Seattle art studio to help my grandmother when she became ill. Doctors diagnosed her with Stage 4 terminal stomach cancer.

While Gigi was resting after chemotherapy treatment, she said, "Making the jam will be too much for you at this point, but maybe someday you can tackle it."

When she passed away, we cried for days, my aunt, my cousin, and her customers in town. And then we did what she had asked. We kept going without her. But that doesn't stop me from aching for her loving arms while I roll out quiche crusts and push pans laden with scones into the oven.

I wipe my eyes with the back of my hand.

"What's going on?" Lydia says. "You thinking about Gigi?"

I nod and give her arm a squeeze. By putting off inventorying every drawer and purging paperwork, I've kept remnants of Gigi around me. As a child, I'd stay awake missing my parents and wishing they were alive. My grandmother's footsteps coming down the hall reassured me with each soft step of a slipper.

"Go to sleep," she said from the doorway. "I'll be here tomorrow. You can count on that."

But now I don't have her to rely on. I've got Aunt Jean and Lydia, and that's it. I left behind anyone who cared for me in Seattle.

5

I drive up a hill landscaped with salal and lavender plants and stop at a security guard shack. A metal archway above the paved road displays a sign for Field Estates.

The guard steps away from a fan and leans out the window. He's in his early twenties, and his face is flushed. Sweat beads on his upper lip. It must be stinking hot in the booth.

"Who are you here to see?"

Lydia leans over. "Boots Brinker."

"She expecting you?"

"Not so much, but she knows who I am. Tell her Lydia wants to see her."

He wipes his brow with the back of his hand.

"Go on ahead. They told me they were expecting a

large crowd for their party today, and some might not be on the list."

Lydia says, "Which house is it?"

He points left. "The big one with pillars looking over the valley. You'll see a round stained-glass window on the second floor."

I wiggle my fingers in a goodbye. "Okay, thanks."

Snaking up the road to the left, we pass houses big enough to hold three or more of my grandmother's home. With a stab in the gut, I remember. Her place is mine now.

"Whoa," Shane says from the back seat. "Look at these gargantuan houses. They're not messing around, are they? No expenses spared. That one must be eight thousand square feet or more."

I smile. His voice reminds me of a time when I was young and optimistic.

I say, "They'd have to call each on their cells to find each other in all that space."

"I bet they text," Lydia says.

"Or both," Shane adds, ever the peacemaker.

Each house has a distinct look, but the landscaping is similar, with rock gardens and grasses. On our right, a two-story Tudor with stucco siding and brown trim has an attached four-car garage with a carriage house above. If Lydia lived there, she'd sneak off to the garage apartment to be alone with Shane.

I shake my head to clear my mind and focus on the

present task. One is to interrogate Boots. Two, I'll see if she has the item in question. I also want to interview her brother and dad about what they saw yesterday afternoon at the café. Three, if they have it, take the diary and get out of there fast. Four, I'll go home and read the journal with my feet up while sipping a fresh cup of strong coffee. Five, I'll deal with any surprises I find in the pages. I'll accept the bigger picture of who my grandmother was and move on.

My plan sounds deceptively easy. But something inside me taps out a warning. I have a feeling that this won't be as straight-forward as throwing a bowl on the potter's wheel. I have a hunch a puzzle awaits, and I'll have to figure it out.

We come to a modern home with a copper roof and copper gutters.

Shane whistles. "I can't imagine how much that cost to build."

A round stained-glass window on the second floor means we've arrived. Party music blares from a pool area. Cars fill the driveway and line the street.

I pull over and park.

"Can't wait to see this place," Shane says, hopping out. "Thanks for inviting me."

I smile. His enthusiasm is refreshing, like a sea breeze after a storm. I'd like to bathe in it and wash off the tired, cynical version of myself that I've become. I didn't expect Gigi to live forever, but her death caught me by surprise. I'd thought we had many more years left together.

Lydia slams the car door. "Remember," she says to me and linking her arm with Shane's, "let me introduce you before you bring up the journal. You can't just dive in and demand something. We've got to establish a relationship first and create trust."

I nod. Perhaps she is more mature than I realized. "You're right. Roger that."

Following a flagstone path, I'm taken aback by the wealth on display. This cluster of homes didn't exist when I was growing up. Standing on the front step, I ring the doorbell.

Chimes sound inside.

My hands clench. I take a deep breath. Gigi's journal is forcing me out in the world, hunting for it, when I'd rather be working in clay all by myself.

Mr. Brinker opens the door. His silver hair is as movie-star perfect as ever. He says, "There you are, good to see you. Come inside and join the party."

My stomach knots. I avoid groups and haven't mastered the art of small talk.

I manage to say, "Thanks."

Layla smiles. "Hi, Mr. Brinker. Good to see you."

Shane sticks out his hand. "I'm Shane. Nice to meet you."

"Bob Brinker. Come on in." He ushers us inside. "Boots and Guns are by the pool. Grab a refreshment and go on out. They'll be glad to see you."

Lydia heads for the grand kitchen and pours herself a rum and Coke.

There's a butler's pantry, two stainless-steel six-burner Viking ranges, two ovens, a warming oven and two dishwashers. I moan with envy. What I wouldn't give to work in this space. If I had enough money, I'd remodel Gigi's kitchen.

I say to Lydia, "This is a kitchen to die for, isn't it?"

She sips her drink. "I could get used to living here."

"Me too," I say. "But it might feel too big after a while." I take the red plastic cup from her. "You're too young to be drinking rum, especially at this time of day."

She fixes me with a hard look when I pour her drink down the drain. I wouldn't mind a glass of wine to take the edge off. But I need my mind to be clear when I ask Boots if she took the journal or saw someone else take it.

"How about ginger ale instead?" I say.

I babysat her when she was little, and after dinner, I made ginger ale floats with vanilla ice cream.

She shrugs. "Sure, that works."

Shane finds us as we're leaving the kitchen, carrying cans of ginger ale. "This is some place," he says.

We head out to the pool and stand on the fringes of a group of about twenty people in sundresses and shirts over swim trunks. Boots is at the center of the group. Her long jet-black hair shines in the sun, unlike my limp, dull pink hair. She's wearing huge white-rimmed sunglasses and looks very much at ease.

Boots gives Shane a smile. "I'm glad to see you here." She turns to Lydia and me. "We bumped into each other at a coffee shop the other day."

Lydia frowns for a flicker of a second. "Hi, Boots, my cousin is looking for something you might have." She puts her hands on her hips. "Did you take the diary from her dining room?"

I flinch at Lydia's accusing tone. She must be jealous of the attention Boots is giving to Shane. To intervene, I step forward. My pulse picks up. Gigi would be furious if she knew I had let her journal leave the house.

"Sorry to barge in," I say. "But I can't find my grandmother's diary. And I've got to get it back. Did you take it with you by mistake?"

I pose it as a question. But it's not. I'm here to get my property back, and that's a fact.

Boots sips a drink. "I know you, from the café and from school."

I nod. "The journal is missing. Do you happen to know where it is?"

She taps a finger to her lips. "I left it on the table, like you said to." She turns to Lydia. "I didn't take it, so don't accuse me." She bats her eyelashes at Shane.

We are getting three versions of Boots. The sincere adult for me, the girl-fighter don't mess with me for Lydia, and the come-hither option for Shane.

Boots says, "I'm an econ major, and I would like to write a paper about the impact of a stock market crash on human behavior. Gigi's notebook would be an excellent resource to use in my research. I don't have it, but when you do find it, I'd like to read it right away."

Arching an eyebrow, I cross my arms. Diaries should be private, and not shared with people who want to paw through the pages and publicize personal entries. Her asking to read it before I've had a chance to peruse the contents takes a lot of nerve.

I check her over, looking for a twitching cheek muscle or fidgeting hands, in case she lied, and she's hiding the journal. She looks at me and doesn't blink. I'm not completely sure, but I have the feeling that Boots is innocent.

I hold out my phone. "Give me your number, in case I find it and decide to share it."

She taps in her cell number.

Taking the phone back, I say, "Did you see anyone who might've taken it? Did someone walk by the table and ask about it?"

Lydia takes Shane by the hand, and they walk to the edge of the pool.

Boots leans in. "He's a dish, isn't he? I'd love to go out with him, but he doesn't seem interested."

"I know what you mean. Now about the journal?"

"Oh, right." She studies the blue sky for a moment. "Wanda Robinson passed through the dining room on her way to the restroom. She asked about it. And when we left, Mr. Frackus, the science teacher, picked up something that looked like it came from the diary. It was a ripped page."

My pulse quickens. I'm on the hunt and getting closer to finding the journal.

"I'll find Mr. Frackus. Do you know Wanda, or have her number?"

"Nope. But I bet my brother does." She says, "Guns, get over here."

Guns saunters over. He's dressed in black and the only one in the group who is wearing long pants and a long-sleeved shirt. He has on gold eyeliner. His hair is pulled back in a ponytail.

"What's the situation? If you need an actor, I'm your man."

Boots grins and slaps his arm. "This isn't about a gig. It's about the red notebook at the café."

I smile. Their playful connection makes me wish I had a sibling. Someone who'd have my back and who would be there for me when everyone else takes off.

She says to her brother, "Karina wants to get in touch with Wanda. Do you have her number?"

Guns says, "She was in my acting class. She said improv helps her write dialogue."

Boots scuffs a bejeweled flip flop on the patio. "Karina wants to ask her about the journal."

Guns shrugs. "I don't know her cell. You should go to the store and ask Mr. Robinson."

He looks over at Lydia, who is sitting by the pool, dangling her feet.

I hand him my business card. "If you remember her number, call me or stop by the cafe."

He nods and wanders over to a group by the pool.

I turn to his sister. "Thanks, Boots. Let me know if you remember anything else."

On the way out, we pass Mr. Brinker in the living room. He's standing at a wet bar and pouring a draft beer from the tap into a frosted glass. I guess he's rich enough to own his own keg. His company develops software that tracks pharmacy inventories, and Gigi said he knew everyone in town.

Shane comes to a stop. "You have your own keg?"

Brinker smiles. "Work hard, and you could have a set up like this one day."

Shane nods. "I intend to. What brand of beer is it, if I may ask?"

"Stella. The kids tried to get into my supply of hard booze, so I had to lock it up. They don't drink my beer. Usually." He steals a glance out back to the party, where his daughter is throwing his son, fully clothed, into the pool. He chuckles. "Never sure if they are fighting or getting along, those two."

I say, "After I closed the café yesterday, Gigi's red journal ended up missing. Did you see anyone take it when you were there?"

He fingers his chin. "Kenny Robinson was interested

in it. So was his daughter, Wanda, who finished her master's degree. He's really proud of her. Wish my kids were that driven."

"They strike me as motivated," I say, "as long as it's about economics and acting."

He looks down at his boat shoes. When I was growing up, we couldn't afford those or the clothes that kids in town wore. Gigi and I frequented thrift stores before it became popular.

"I was hoping they'd join me in the family business," he says with a frown. "But they're not interested."

"They might come around," Shane says. "Or Lydia could take over when she grows up. She likes bossing people around."

"I'm grown up," Lydia says, glaring at him. "And I'm not bossy, I'm direct." To Brinker, she says, "I'd like to work for your company, if you need part-time help."

I furrow my brow. "But you work for me. We're family. We stick together."

"I'm not tied to you. I'm free to explore other options."

My hand flies to my chest. I had assumed she'd work for me until she finished high school. She is my only employee, and I'll be short-handed without her help.

She turns to Brinker. "Your employees look happy when they go into work. I've noticed that when I'm walking to high school. Gigi said your business keeps track of medications used in long-term care centers and hospitals. That sounds interesting."

My face heats. I can't believe she's bailing on me. I did her a favor by hiring her and being lenient. Now, she's going to ditch me for something better.

Pulling out a business card, Brinker gives it to her.

"I like your attitude. Give me a call this week, and we'll set up an interview."

Lydia grins, holding the card in two hands like it's precious. And it is. She spoke her truth and it opened a door to her future, leaving me to bake egg pies on my own.

She beams. "Thank you so much. I'm Lydia. Lydia Barker."

He chuckles. "I know. I've seen you at the café."

As we head to the car, I mull over how I'm going to find time to hire a new assistant and track down the journal. I roll my eyes. Life isn't always easy, and I'd better buckle up and get tough.

I review my plan for recovering the diary. I need to speak with Kenny Robinson and ask him for his daughter's contact information. If he won't tell me, I'll check every Starbucks in the area. I bet I'll find her hunched over a laptop, writing a novel, and nursing a cup of chai tea.

I have nothing to offer in exchange for Gigi's journal, but I must get it back.

6

On the ride home, Lydia and Shane offer to wash the pots and pans at the café. I thank them, drop them off at the house, and head over to Kenny's Sporting Goods near the marina. I hope Kenny Robinson will be in, because I want to get his daughter's phone number and learn if he knows anything about the diary's whereabouts.

Climbing out of my four-door Honda sedan, I take a deep breath. Salt air wafts past from Cedar Channel. As the smell of the Salish Sea welcomes me home, my tense back muscles loosen. It would be great if this one visit would solve my problem and end the hunt for the notebook. Maybe Kenny Robinson will pull it out of his desk drawer and hand it over.

I roll my eyes and tell myself to stop dreaming and get

going. Gigi wanted me to read the journal, so I'd better find it fast and get back to running her business, just like she asked me to. I let out a sigh and stroll to the store entrance. Following in my grandmother's footsteps is much tougher than I thought it would be when I sat on her bed and held her hand on her last night.

I enter the store, and a bell rings. The place smells like new shoes. Stopping at the counter, I ask for Mr. Robinson.

The middle-aged salesperson wrinkles her nose. "Is he expecting you?"

"No, but he'll want to see me."

The truth is, I'm desperate. Losing the journal has made me more aware of Gigi's passing. During the day when no one is around and a board creaks, I hope it's her. Then I reach for a tissue and have a good cry.

The salesperson picks up a hand-held two-way radio.

"Mr. Robinson, a young woman's here to see you."

Kenny Robinson comes out of the storeroom door. Gigi's scones have given him a paunch. He's six feet tall with a linebacker's build. He played football in high school. Purple and orange Millersville High Movers pennants hang on the wall.

"Hi Karina, how can I help you?" he says.

"I wanted to thank you for coming in with your family yesterday and to ask about an item that's gone missing."

His bushy eyebrows furrow. He crosses his arms. "And what might that be?"

My heart thuds. He's defensive and acting like I've irritated him. But I plow ahead.

"My grandmother's diary was in the dining room. Boots Brinker left it on the table. But I can't find it, and I wondered if your daughter, Wanda, might've taken it by chance? I'm following leads to get it back. Wanda apparently asked Boots about the journal when she went to the restroom?"

I bite my lip. My voice went up at the end of the sentence. I've got to stop doing that.

He takes a step back. "You were misled if you think my daughter had anything to do with this. Wanda mentioned the book. I'm a history buff, and I wanted to look it over. But she would never, and I mean never, take anything that doesn't belong to her. After we ate, I paid the bill, and we left."

Kenny frowns. He's one of Gigi's best customers. I don't want word getting out around town that I'm accusing customers of stealing. That would kill Gigi's business, which is all I've got left of her.

He clears his throat. "Are you accusing my family of taking something?"

"Oh gosh, no. I'm sorry I gave you that impression. It's just that I don't know where to look, and I'm pretty shaken up about it. It was Gigi's, and it means a lot to me. She asked me to read it right before she died. It's vitally important that I find it. What would you do if you were in my position? Where would you look?"

His hands drop to his sides. "I understand, and I'd be happy to help you search. It sounds like Gigi meant for you to read whatever she wrote in it. By the way, when you find it, I'd like to examine the notebook."

I rub my lips. It seems everyone wants to read what my grandmother wrote.

He says, "Let's go over your search so far and talk about what you might do next." He counts on his fingers. "You've spoken with Boots. Now you've asked me. You'll want to talk with Wanda, in case she saw something. If I were you, I'd make a list of all the people who were at the café yesterday afternoon."

"That's almost impossible," I say, holding up my hands, "given how busy it was. But I'll see what I can come up with."

"Bob Brinker and his kids were there. We were. While I was paying the bill, a tall, broad-shouldered man came inside and left a few minutes later. He was in his thirties, I'd guess. He could've grabbed it. He was wearing a flannel shirt, a tweed cap, and a green raincoat. Do you know who he is?"

Shaking my head, I say, "I don't know who that might be. I had an order to go right about then for an older gentleman who moved here with his wife, who is ill. He wanted two cranberry scones and two slices of quiche. The person you described sounds like my cousin's boyfriend, Shane. He's tall, but he's younger than that. I'll ask him if he saw anything unusual."

Kenny stabs the air with an index finger. "Ah hah. Problem solved. Shane is the culprit. He must've taken it."

Sweat beads on his brow. He's deflecting attention by accusing Shane. Maybe Kenny is guilty and pocketed the diary. I'll have to keep my eyes out and monitor everyone who might have a motive.

"I doubt it," I say, "but I'll talk to him. Let's not jump to conclusions. How can I reach your daughter?"

He tells me Wanda's cell number, and I say, "Thanks. And I'd like to speak with your wife, in case she saw something and didn't mention it?"

I purse my lips. There I am, doing that upspeak again at the end of a sentence.

He shrugs. "Sure, go ahead and stop by the house if you like. We're at the corner of M and 6th, in the big white house on the corner. My younger daughter Maddie likes you."

"She's a great kid."

I have a bounce in my step as I head to the car. Now I'm getting somewhere. But I stop when I spot a note tucked under my windshield wiper. Pulling it out, I read the typed words.

"Stop looking. You won't find it."

Gritting my teeth, I scan the parking lot, which is empty except for a few cars. A paper cup skitters across the pavement, carried by the breeze. I crumple the note and toss it on the passenger seat.

Climbing in, I sit back with a sigh. Secrets call from Gigi's notebook. I was remiss to let it out of my sight.

She wanted me to read the diary. For Gigi's sake, I'll pursue every lead to recover the journal. And I'll keep the café open. I won't renege on my promise to my much-missed guardian.

7

On the way home, I swing by the Robinsons' big white house at the corner of M and 6th. A badminton net is strung across the front lawn. Shouts come from a side yard. A soccer ball bounces out, heading for the street.

I catch the ball and toss it to Maddie. Her cheeks are rosy, and her hair is in pigtails.

"Here you go. Is your mom home?"

She smiles. She's missing an upper front tooth. "You're Karina, the quiche lady. I'm the one who asks for extra jam. Your jam tastes delectable."

"Thanks. My grandma made it herself. Delectable is a big word for you to use."

She grins. "I'm practicing for the spelling bee."

"I hope you'll win. It sounds like you know your stuff."

She hugs the ball to her stomach and eyes me. "It's not about winning. It's about participating and doing your best."

I shrug, feeling chastised by a child, and say, "You're absolutely right. Hey, listen, I'm trying my best to find something that disappeared from the café yesterday. I'd like to talk with your mom and see if she knows anything about it."

When I head for the blue front door, Maddie follows along behind.

"Did you lose it?" she says. "Is it your fault? My mom says it's best to own up to your mistakes and not lie or cover them up."

Children's voices holler in the side yard. "Maddie, bring the ball back! We want to play."

"Just a minute," she calls. "Well?"

I smile. This kid is precocious. I bend down so we're at eye level.

"I lost my grandmother's journal, and I'm trying to find it."

"Maybe I can help," Maddie says. Her breath smells like an orange popsicle.

The front door opens. Ellie Robinson, in a red sweater and yoga pants, stares.

I've been attracting scrutiny since moving home from the city and getting the can-I-trust you look that comes with raised eyebrows. I'm not the girl who left after college wearing a high ponytail. Black leather pants, a pierced nose, and pink hair shouldn't be a big deal. But in my small town, it is.

"What were you talking to my daughter about?"

My fingers make a puzzle in front of me, wiggling to find comfort. I clear my throat. I'm suddenly eight years old and being bawled out by a neighbor for kicking the ball into a plate glass window. Gigi backed me up and said we all make mistakes. She patted my back and told the neighbor I was just a child and not to be so harsh. She'd pay to replace the window. I worked in the kitchen after that, helping to make scones to pay Gigi back.

"I'm Karina, who runs the quiche café?" I frown and tell myself to snap out of it. I'm not a child. I am a grown woman. "I'm looking for a diary that went missing from Gigi's while you were there?"

She crosses her arms. "Are you accusing us of taking it? If you are, we won't patronize your shop anymore."

My hands flutter as if they're trying to fly away. I'd better explain fast, or my reputation will be ruined, and my restaurant will be empty. My grandmother will be pointing a finger at me and frowning from wherever she is.

"Not at all. I'll start over and explain. My grandmother's journal is missing, and I have no idea where it is. I'm asking everyone who was there yesterday afternoon if they might've seen someone take the diary."

She tilts her head. I'm not sure if she's going to invite

me in or close the door in my face. The café will be dead. The seconds slog by.

"We've frequented Gigi's Café for years, and your grandmother was like family. But you need to learn to communicate better, or you'll turn the whole town against you, do you understand?"

I swallow hard. "Yes, I do, and I appreciate your advice. It's something I'm working on and know I need to improve. Gigi scolded me for my blabber mouth."

She chuckles. "I heard her bawling you out in the kitchen once for telling a customer two scones were enough for one person. The rest were for other guests."

I nod. "I said that when I was younger. And I'm not exactly smooth now at operating the café. It's a huge responsibility. I was working at an art studio in Seattle when my aunt called and said Gigi was fading." I dab at my leaking eyes.

Her eyebrows furrow. "Oh, dear. I had no idea. Would you like to come in for a cup of tea? Maybe we could come up with a list of the people who were there yesterday afternoon."

I'm not a tea drinker, but I could use her help, and I want to find out what she knows. If I can finagle a way to search for the diary while I'm here, I'd like to do that. Then I'd either end the hunt and go home with the item in question or eliminate the Robinsons from the list of suspects. I feel bad about the idea of sneaking around, and I know my grandmother wouldn't approve, but I'm pulled toward wherever they keep their papers. I'll start in the study, if they have one.

"Thanks, I would. May I use your bathroom?"

She motions me inside. "Of course, the downstairs powder room is to your right. I'll see you in the kitchen. And you can call me Ellie."

I cringe as I disappear into the restroom. Glancing in the mirror, I may look the same, but inside I'm changing. My desperate hunt to recover the notebook is driving me to deceive someone who is helping me. She trusts me and invited me into her home.

I gulp at my ease in putting up a false front. Whatever it takes to get the notebook back. If I find it here, I'll have taken the correct course of action.

After I use the facilities, I tiptoe on the dark floorboards to the far side of the house, guided by instinct. I enter a study with a large mahogany desk situated on a red area rug. Two leather arm chairs sit opposite the desk. The furnishings in the room look plush and like they have expensive tastes.

My pulse quickens. A headache throbs. I clamp my teeth together and get to work. I only have a few moments to look. But a strong urge to stride out of the room hits me. My grandmother's scolding voice is almost shouting in my head. I shouldn't be doing this. It isn't right.

All the same, I shake it off and scan the desk top. Two piles of papers are neatly stacked. The leather-bound blotter is bare. There's no sign of my grandmother's diary.

I open a drawer. No red journal. Just paper clips, pens, and a ruler.

With a sigh, I decide to give it up. But then my cheeks heat with shame. I'm trespassing in their home in my hunger to recover a family memento. It dawns on me that I am doing is against the law.

I drum my fingers on the blotter. My strong motivation and emotional attachment to the notebook doesn't make it okay to invade other people's personal spaces. This is the last time I'll cross a legal line to get back what is mine.

I flinch when I hear quick footsteps padding down the hallway. I have got to get out of this room and go find Ellie in the kitchen.

"What're you doing in here?" Maddie says. "Shouldn't you be in the kitchen?"

My palms turn cold. I put a finger to my lips and head for the door.

"I'm going to tell my mother."

"Please, don't. I need her on my side. If you keep quiet, I'll give you extra jam. Until it runs out, that is."

She tilts her head. "Why's it going to run out?"

Going toward the kitchen, I say, "Gigi made it. I haven't had the courage to try to follow her recipe. Or the time."

"Be courageous," she says. "You've got to try new things. Get out of habits that make you feel comfortable."

I pat her shoulder. Her parents must have coached her. "That's very wise."

We enter a large, modern kitchen with white

cupboards. Slabs of white quartz cover the countertops and two islands. A blue tile backsplash in a geometric pattern matches the color of the front door. Stainless appliances shine. I eye a six-burner stove top, two ovens, and two dishwashers. If only this was mine.

"Found her," Maddie says. "I guess she got lost."

8

Ellie Robinson gestures to a barstool. "Go ahead and sit down. I'll pour the tea."

I sink onto a stool and vow to be a better person. I'll earn the town's trust and show them I belong back here, running a revered local institution.

I say, "Thanks for taking time. I appreciate it."

When her back is turned, I whisper to Maddie, "Thanks for covering for me."

Maddie takes three sugar cookies and runs outside. "Cookies!"

"Your daughter is something else," I say. "It must be challenging to raise a child that bright."

Ellie sets down two mugs of tea.

"She takes after me. Bubble tests are easy for us. You know, the standardized ones? They're fun to fill in, and we ace them."

"You're lucky. I wasn't the best student. I'm better with my hands and working in clay or painting. But I did go to college."

Her head cocks. She watches me, as if she's a bird, and I'm a worm. "What was your degree in? Mine's in history, and I went on to get a law degree. I work remotely and have my own law firm."

No wonder their kitchen is so decked out.

I shrug. "Art. I make sculptures and throw pots on the wheel. In Seattle, I did art shows and sold my work. Now I run the café."

She pats the island countertop, and her diamond ring sparkles.

"That's a big life change. Well, welcome back to town. You're working hard, and Gigi would be proud of you. Now tell me about the diary. We'll brainstorm who was there when it went missing. And go ahead, help yourself to a cookie."

She sounds like a problem solver, and I could use the help of a results-oriented person who knows everyone in town.

Taking a sip of Darjeeling tea, I set the cup down. "I like the tea. And thanks for inviting me in. So, as you know, it was crazy at the café yesterday afternoon. Orders were backed up, and I was hurrying around because my cousin flaked out on me. She up and left in the middle of a rush."

"That's Lydia, isn't it? And she's dating Shane, who is

quite a bit older?"

I nod. No one keeps secrets for long in my hometown.

"Shane is in college," I say. "And my aunt doesn't approve of the age gap."

"I agree. I'd never let Maddie do that. And I wouldn't have let Wanda either when she was Lydia's age."

"She's about to graduate, and she thinks she knows everything."

Ellie rolls her eyes and snorts. "I remember feeling like that."

I chuckle. "Me too. So, back to the diary, when the Brinkers were waiting in the dining room, Boots opened a drawer. She found a journal and showed me a page where Gigi wrote about a Monday when the stock market crashed in 1987. Apparently she took money out of the bank and hid it."

I hold up my hands. "I didn't even know the journal was there. I was meaning to look for it, but I've been too busy. Things have been crazy at the café."

Biting a fingernail, I wonder if I can ever begin to run the restaurant smoothly, like I promised. And if I'll get the diary back, what will I read in the pages? Will I find secrets or will it be a dull account of daily chores, meant to guide me as the café's new manager?

Ellie says, "You know, I did see Mr. Frackus outside when we left. But I didn't see him go in." She pushed the plate of cookies closer to me. "Now, go on, try a molasses cookie. They're from the Bread Farm Bakery and really good."

I bite into one, and coarse sugar melts on my tongue. A tang of ginger makes my taste buds wake up. Mr. Frackus's name keeps coming up. I need to track him down and talk to him next.

Ellie says, "But are you sure the diary was Gigi's?"

I nod. "I'm sure, because it was my grandmother's handwriting. But it might be part of a puzzle she meant for me to find. When I was young, she'd make up games for me with clues. It'd take weeks for me to solve them and find the hidden treasure. I wonder if her journal has clues like that."

I eat another cookie and wash it down with tea.

She taps a finger to her lips. "If you found the money, what would you do with it?"

"Pay off my student loans. Fix the roof. Remodel the kitchen, if there's enough."

She gestures to the grand kitchen, which opens onto a patio and the back yard. "I can recommend a designer if you need one."

I tilt my head. "I'm more of a do-it-yourself kind of person, but thanks."

She says, "What was Boots doing anyway, going through your personal things?"

My face heats, recalling how I riffled through the desk in their study. "I don't know, and I wish she hadn't. Maybe she was bored. They were waiting a while for service. Do you remember anyone else who was there besides the Brinkers and your family?"

"A man with a newsboy cap down over his eyes came in and left right away."

I chew on my lower lip. "I didn't see him."

"It was busy at the time. Maybe he couldn't get your attention to place an order, so he decided to leave."

I blow out a breath. If Lydia hadn't left me alone in the café with a crowd, I wouldn't be going around town searching for Gigi's journal. Guests would have been served promptly yesterday and given more attention. Boots would not have had time to open a built-in drawer in the private dining room.

Maddie comes in the back door. "Going to the bathroom. Bye."

"Walk, don't run," Ellie says in a firm voice.

Maddie slows to a trot. "K."

Leaning in, I say, "The man with the newsboy cap, what color was it? How old was he?"

She taps her red manicured nail, which matches her sweater, on the counter. "Maybe thirty. I'm not sure. I couldn't see his face. He went to the bathroom and walked out right away. He kept his head down."

Now we're getting somewhere. "What kind of jacket? What color was it?"

"A green, zip-up REI type raincoat. The kind that's got a hood and goes down to your knees? He hunched over when he left. What bothered me was it wasn't raining. Why would anyone wear a coat like that on a sunny day?"

"That's odd. I'll look into it. Did you see him talk to anyone?"

"He whispered something to Wanda as she passed him."

"She's on my list of people to talk to. Do you think Mr. Frackus would have any reason to be interested in my grandmother's journal?"

She waves a hand. "I don't think so. He's retired. Everyone had him for science class in high school, didn't they? He wouldn't be interested in a diary."

She looks at me, and her eyes light up. "But there was a couple in the front room, now that I think of it. You know that man with a dragon tattoo on his neck? Zerk? He and Bets just moved here, and they work at the Brown Lantern?"

I smile. "That's right. I'd forgotten about them. Thanks. I'll go talk to them."

I stand and give her my card that says, "Gigi's Café, where you'll leave with a smile after a home-cooked meal. We serve decent food with fabulous service."

I frown. Yesterday, I let customers down. Any idea of excellent service evaporated when Lydia walked out the door to run a fake errand in the midst of a record-setting crowd. I must be firm with her. But the trouble is, I'm not used to being a boss. Besides, she's my cousin, and I want her to like me. I have a lot to learn about running my own business.

I say, "Thanks, you've been really helpful. Please call or text me if you think of anything else."

"I will, and good luck. It sounds like it means a lot to you."

"I had no idea Gigi kept a journal. Reading it would be like getting to know a new side of her." I wipe a tear from my eye.

Maddie appears. "Could I have a card? I'll help you investigate."

This kid is so cute, she makes me smile. I hand her a business card and say to them, "Get in touch if you think of a detail I missed. Thanks."

I head out to my car. I've got to get in touch with Mr. Frackus. People keep mentioning his name. I doubt my former high school science teacher had anything to do with the notebook's disappearance, but I need to follow every lead.

9

I swing by the Brown Lantern on the way home to speak with Bets and Zerk. A band is setting up. A guitarist is strumming his instrument and testing the microphone. The drummer reminds me of my former boyfriend, Jeff, in Seattle. He leans over the drum set and pounds out a beat without looking up.

Sports jerseys hang on the wall and wooden ceiling. Framed photos show athletes holding up awards. Football teams line up in group shots. A fat tire bike hangs from the ceiling. This is my kind of place. I need to come here and hang out when I get my life in order.

Behind the bar is Zerk, the bartender, with a dragon tattoo on his neck.

I slide onto a barstool, and he grins.

He says, "What'll it be, Karina who runs the cafe? It is my turn to serve you."

I drum my fingers on the smooth wood bar top, considering my options. It's been a few months since I've gone out for a drink. I've been cooped up inside.

"I'll take a Negroni," I say. "Thanks."

He beams. "I can make that. Coming right up."

"But wait," I say, holding up an index finger. "I think my tastes have changed."

His face falls. "All right."

"I think I'd like to try something new. Maybe not too wild. Not beer either, I'm not in the mood for that today."

He points a finger at me and says, "I know just what you need. How's a gin gimlet sound? Or, better yet, a vodka gimlet. It needs to be cold and strong, and the lime juice in it will stave off scurvy, if you're a sailor stuck on a boat at sea for months, back in the day."

I smile. "Yes, I'll have a vodka gimlet. It can be my new drink."

He mixes my drink, and his wife, Bets, breezes past. She waitresses and bartends here. The two carry an aura of mystery and don't talk much about where they came from. But I guess everyone deserves to have secrets.

When they come into Gigi's Café, they take their coffee hot and black but skip slathering Gigi's jam on scones. Sometimes they stop in with Harold Biggins, but he usually hangs out at Dad's Diner, which is my competition. There's plenty of business for everyone, so I don't sweat it if Harold or Bets or Zerk two-time me and have breakfast somewhere else.

A man in a brown Carhart jacket is on my left at the bar.

Bets serves him a bowl of chili. "There you go. Anything else?"

"Another glass of that pinot noir, but not the house one."

"Sure thing."

Bets fills his glass in a flash, sets it down and turns to me.

"Karina, what brings you in? I never see you out of your café."

I shrug. "It's time I got out and mixed, but I'd rather it be under different circumstances."

She leans in. "What do you mean?"

"Gigi's journal disappeared yesterday from the café. I can't find it, so I'm asking around to see if anyone saw someone take it."

"Is it valuable?"

I cringe when I see a glint in her eyes, recalling what I overhead about their leaving a life of crime. I really like Bets, but at this point, I don't trust anyone.

"No, it's not valuable at all," I say. "It's a sentimental item that was my grandmother's and only special to me. It's just a bunch of personal thoughts that wouldn't mean anything to someone other than family. No one else would want it."

Zerk sets a gimlet in front of me. "Here you go. A drink for a special young lady. Taste it and see what you think."

I take a sip, and my taste buds spring to life. "I like it. This is perfect."

He puts his hands together. "Excellent. Nice to see you out exploring the world beyond your café."

"Hon," Bets pats his arm. "A notebook is missing from her place, and she's looking for it."

Zerk frowns. "That's too bad."

Setting my drink down, I say, "When you were in the café yesterday, did you happen to notice any questionable activity or suspicious people, by chance?"

They look at each other and laugh. She punches his arm playfully and grins. Turning to me, she says, "Other than us, nope. No one suspicious."

Zerk holds up a finger. "What about the guy in the green raincoat on a sunny day? What was that about? I'd look into him if I were you."

The man next to me puts down his chili spoon. "A guy in a green raincoat? It could be anyone of a hundred men in town. Good luck finding him." He laughs.

I nod. "You're right." My search may be fruitless, but I've got to try.

Just then, Violet walks in the door and looks around.

I wave to her, and she comes over. I gesture to the open barstool on my right. "Take a seat, unless you're waiting for someone."

"Nope, no one is joining me," she says, sliding onto the barstool. "I'm on my own."

Every move she makes is stealthy as a cat. No wonder

she is an expert at surveillance and corporate security. No one would see her coming. I'm guessing she is five or ten years older than me, and I sense we could be friends. Something about her is familiar, but I can't place it.

I say, "We can finally get that drink together we've been meaning to schedule."

Violet whooshes out a breath. "Work has been non-stop. I have three clients now. How's it going for you?"

"About the same," I say, "I'm running in place. These are wild times. Everyone wants a scone or a slice of quiche and, apparently, protection from Outrigger Services."

She nods and looks ahead at the glittering liquor bottles on the bar.

I study the bump on her nose that supposedly resembles mine. I don't think we look anything alike, but perhaps if I saw my doppelganger, I wouldn't recognize her.

Zerk calls out, "Bar back, we need to change the keg."

A bearded guy says, "Got it." He mumbles about air in the line and strides to the back.

Zerk thumps on the bar with a hand and says to Violet, "What'll it be for the woman who saved our town and protected Brinker's company?"

Violet grins. "A pilsner, thanks."

He says, "Tell you what, it'll be on the house today."

He sets a cold glass of beer down on a coaster in front of her. "We appreciate what you did. It could've been much worse." He cocks his head. "Of course, there was your mother on the other side. That was something. She is a formidable foe, I'd say."

Bets comes by, swatting his arm. "Let them talk. Don't hover and bore them."

He smiles. "I was never one to pass up a captive audience. I'll check with you later." He moves down the bar and washes glasses.

I sip my drink and try to recall the last time I hung out with anyone, having a casual conversation. No instance comes to mind. I spent my time in the city making art, and I didn't have much money. Now I have a bit more money, but no time for art. I sigh.

Violet hunches over and says in a low voice, "Speaking of family, and reminded of my mother, I've been meaning to ask you something."

She sounds secretive. I give her a close look, but she won't meet my eyes. She runs a finger over the frosted glass. A trail of condensation trickles down onto the coaster.

"Go ahead," I say. "Ask me anything. I'm an open book. What is it?"

She opens her mouth, but whatever she was about to say is swept away in a blast of laughter from three people entering the bar.

"There's our boss," Vincent says, coming over.

Mimi says, "We thought we'd find her here. Let's get a table."

She claps Violet on the back.

Violet says, "Hey, guys."

She says to me, "We'll continue this conversation later. Care to join us?"

"Thanks," I say, "but I think I'll finish this drink and head home. I have a lot to do, and I have to get up early tomorrow."

Sipping my drink, I nod to myself in the bar mirror behind many bottles. This isn't the best time for me to mix it up and socialize. I'm grieving my grandmother's death, obsessed with locating her diary, and overwhelmed in the café. In the future, I hope to step into Gigi's shoes and sail through the day, like she did.

But right now, I'm clinging by my finger nails to the little stability I have. What I've gone through would be too much change for anyone, with moving, the death of a loved one, taking over the family business, and hunting down a missing precious item. I just hope I can reclaim the red journal before someone reads it and tracks down the hidden money.

10

I flop onto a pink and green peony patterned sofa at home. Gigi was fond of botanical prints. The colors are jarring, but the couch is comfortable. I kick off my shoes, put my feet up, and tick off the prime suspects on my fingers.

According to Kenny Robinson, Shane came into the café and left soon after. He could have taken the journal.

Boots Brinker, who found the journal, wants to use it for a research paper.

Wanda Robinson, a recent graduate of a writing program, asked about the diary on her way to the restroom. She had the means, motive, and opportunity. Her father could be covering up for her..

Tapping my chin, I add Kenny Robinson to the list. He was keen to get his hands on the diary.

A mysterious man in a green raincoat and newsboy cap came in around the time it went missing.

Mr. Frackus, my high school science teacher, was seen with a page torn out of the diary. Or so people said.

The list is long enough to give me a headache.

The front door opens with a squeal of the hinge. Bells jingle. The door shuts.

"We're closed," I call. "Come back another time."

Footsteps tread on the wood floor.

My heart thumps. I felt safe when Gigi was alive. But now that she's gone, I flinch at every noise. A solitary life in a creaking old house has made me paranoid.

"Who's there?" I say, grabbing a brass candlestick as a weapon and racing down the hall. I stop short. My breath comes in short puffs.

Shane's eyes open wide.

"You scared the scones out of me," I say, "with your sneaking in here."

He glances at the candlestick raised above my head. "I'm looking for Lydia. I thought she might be here. Have you seen her?"

Putting my hands on my hips, I say, "Knock first, next time. Or at least call my name. I wouldn't want to knock you out by mistake. And no, I haven't seen Lydia."

I must start locking the doors while the café is closed. I don't have much that is of value, but I am keeping Gigi's chenille bathrobe with her scent. Her hairbrush is on her dresser, like she left it, on the white embroidered runner that my mother made.

Shane glances toward the kitchen.

I say, "How about a cup of coffee? I have something to discuss with you."

His eyebrows rise. "Sounds serious. But sure, why not?"

While I grind the beans and get the coffee going, he wanders around the kitchen, looking at photos on the walls of Gigi and me when I was young.

"You were a cute kid," he says.

I roll my eyes. "Meaning now I'm a haggard shell of myself, running Gigi's?"

He sits down at the kitchen table. "I wouldn't say haggard. More mature, maybe."

I groan. "Just think what I'll be like in twenty years."

He smiles. "I can see it. A gorgeous beauty, never aging."

I smile at him and feel my stomach flip.

With a beep, the coffee maker announces the coffee is ready.

I turn my back to him and pour two cups of strong coffee. I take a deep breath. It's only Shane, my high school boyfriend. There is no need for me to be nervous.

Setting two cups on the table, I say, "Cream or sugar?"

"Just black."

"So that hasn't changed." I lean forward, closing the gap between us. It's been a long time since we sat this close. He's grown taller. His fingers have calluses now, perhaps from drawing or using tools.

My mind drifts, and I recall years back when I would hold his hand. I shake the thought away.

I clear my throat. "I wanted to say, would you please stop distracting Lydia when the café is open? I need her to help run the place, but she keeps disappearing. It's beyond frustrating. When we were swamped yesterday afternoon, she wasn't here. And because of that, Gigi's journal went missing."

He taps the tabletop. "I can't control what Lydia does, but I'll do my best not to lure her away during work hours. Besides, it sounds like she might not be working here much longer."

I glare at him. "Did she interview with Brinker for the job already?"

"I'm not sure, but she is hell bent on finding a position in a company where she can work her way up."

I sigh. It's not going to be easy to find someone to take her place. Lots of stores in town are looking for part-time help. And I don't want to add another item on my to-do list. It is jam-packed as it is. I want to tell the earth to stop spinning and pause to give me a chance to recover. I want a few days without tons to do, where I'd rest and read the diary and understand my grandmother better.

Shane leans back in the wood chair, and it creaks. "Tell me more about the diary. What did it look like?"

"It has a red leather cover with a gold clasp but no

lock. It's precious because it was Gigi's. I want to read it and discover who she was, besides being my grandmother."

He nods. "That makes sense. I'd feel the same way."

Sitting with him, I'm sixteen again with my future ahead of me. We were innocent back then, except for the hole in my heart after being orphaned. Now my life is mapped out in long stretches of cooking batches of scones, baking quiches, and brewing buckets of coffee. What a grind.

He says, "What are you doing to get it back?"

"I went over to Kenny Robinson's store," I say, "and talked to him about it."

"Remember when we bought a frisbee there?"

His grin makes something sparkle inside me.

I smile. "Your dog destroyed it in a day. But about the journal, Mr. Robinson said you came in and left right away around the time the journal disappeared. Did you take the diary?"

Shane shakes his head. "I didn't do it. I never saw it. I wouldn't steal something, especially not from you. You've had a rough time, with your parents gone and now Gigi too. I wouldn't add to your burden."

He leans forward and takes my hand in his. His hand is warm, and his callouses are rough.

"We had a good thing going," he says, "didn't we?"

My body is bathed in a warm sensation. What feels like a current of electricity runs up my arms. I let out a small sigh. It was just yesterday, when I knew him better than anyone else. But then reality hits. I can't say a word of what is on my mind. He is my cousin's boyfriend. I must tread lightly. After my trespassing in Ellie's study, I want to do the right thing.

I glance up at the ceiling and push away the feeling that my grandmother is watching and listening to our conversation. "We sure did. But that was a long time ago."

Lydia bangs through the back door just then, letting the screen door slap behind her.

Shane drops my hand and shoves his hands in his pockets.

"I've been looking everywhere for you," she says to Shane.

She kisses him, and he ruffles her hair.

She says, "What were you two talking about when I walked in? It looked serious."

"About the diary and how I need your help waiting tables," I say. "Gigi asked me to keep the café going, and I can't do it all by myself."

She picks at a cuticle.

I say, "You've got to show up and stay until your shift ends. You only work after school and on Saturdays anyway."

She frowns. "Fine. I'll show up and hang around until we close. But don't get on my case, or I'll quit. This was all Gigi's dream, not mine. I don't want to make quiches and scones, or serve coffee for the rest of my life."

I blow out an exasperated breath. "This wasn't my dream either. I wanted to have my own art studio in Ballard. But we don't always get to pick our fate."

Shane squirms in his seat. "But I'm doing what I want."

Lydia plops down in his lap.

"Not everyone can," I say to him. "And you're lucky." To Lydia, I say, "Have you heard anyone talking about Gigi's journal? Or has your mom?"

She nods. "My mom says Mr. Rasmus at the library mentioned it. He heard it holds the clues to a mystery, and he'd like to look at it."

I drop my head in my hands. Is there anyone in town who doesn't want to read Gigi's journal?

11

When Lydia and Shane leave, I decide to call Mr. Frackus. His name keeps popping up in my investigation. He probably has a landline, unlike people my age. Taking the White Pages phone book from a shelf, I run my finger down a page, going past Firth and Fritz and back up to Frackus.

There he is, Bernard Frackus on West Elm. There's only one Frackus in the book, so it must be him. I wonder what it was like to grow up with the name of Bernard Frackus. It can't have been easy on the school playground.

His phone number is circled in blue pen, and I didn't do it. Why would Gigi have wanted to speak with my teacher? That's curious.

When I call Mr. Frackus, he doesn't pick up. An answering machine beeps. I leave a message asking him to call me.

Next, I call Wanda Robinson, and she answers.

"Wanda, this is Karina at Gigi's Café. Do you have time to meet? It's about my grandmother's diary."

"My dad said you might call. How about we meet at Starbuck's, the one on Commercial? I'm here writing a short story."

"Great, can we do it now?"

"Give me fifteen minutes. That will be better."

My grip tightens around the phone. She could be writing about Gigi's journal, the one that belongs in my dining room drawer. "What's your story about?"

"Sorry, but I don't discuss stories I'm writing until they're finished. It saps the creative spirit. Ask me in six or eight months."

I nod. Writing isn't like popping scones in the oven, offering instant gratification.

I say, "I'll see you there."

Ten minutes later, I grab my purse and head out, locking the door behind me.

But when I put the key in the ignition, my car doesn't start. My car has one hundred ten thousand miles on it, but I bet it has many more miles left to go. It might just be the battery. I don't want to wait for a tow truck, and I need to go meet Wanda.

My gaze rests on my grandmother's bicycle with a front basket and fat tires. Gigi rode around town shopping and seeing friends. She said bicycling kept her in shape. She was my role model, my hero, and my everything.

I climb out of the car and hop on the bike. I ride with the wind, flying down side streets and pedaling fast. A cool breeze brushes past my cheeks.

I slow to make a turn onto Commercial and rest my foot against the curb.

A car floors it past me, going fast to make the light.

Wind buffets my bike. My arms and legs quiver from an adrenaline rush. I grimace. Vacationers heading to the islands often pass through town in a hurry to get away, catch the ferry, and collapse and relax. With wobbling legs, I continue on.

I stop at Starbuck's and lean the bike against the front window.

Striding inside, I wipe sweat from my brow.

"Is that your bike?" an older woman with short gray hair says. She's reading a book by the window. Ms. Tinsley was the administrative assistant to our high school vice principal, but she must be retired by now. "You should put it in the bike rack."

"I forgot my lock. I want to keep an eye on it."

"You should have a helmet," she says. "This town used to be safe. Back then, you'd leave your bike, and no one would take it. Now we're overrun with strangers, and crime rates are soaring. It's all due to too much growth. That's the problem."

I say, "I grew up here, so I'm not part of the problem."

She stares. "I'm not so sure. You might be a trouble-maker. In fact, I remember you." She scowls.

"Bye, now," I say, spotting Wanda at a table along the wall. She's hunched over her laptop and typing. At the risk of being rude, I sneak up behind her to see what she's writing.

Inhaling a whiff of vanilla bean, cloves, and cinnamon from her chai latte, I read, "Because the journal contained family secrets, she yearned to open it and learn what they were. A deep hunger to know drove her on a path of discovery. Curiosity gnawed at her very being, pulling her closer to the past and the person her grandmother had been."

I take a seat across from her and clear my throat.

She snaps the laptop shut. "Did you read any of it? I hope you didn't. That would be snooping. And I don't like to be watched. It puts me off my rhythm."

"I couldn't help myself. Your story is about Gigi's journal and my search for it, isn't it? It's good. I like the deep hunger and curiosity pulling her closer. But it might have too much telling and not enough showing. But that's just my quick take."

"You think so? Maybe you're right. This is a rough draft. I'll fine tune it later."

She's about my age, but we took different paths. She went to grad school while I worked after college. We both picked fields that don't bring in lots of money, just opportunities for creative expression and personal joy.

I've known her for years. In third grade, she teased me

during recess about my second-hand clothes. I got her back later that day though. On the way home, I pulled off her right shoe and rubbed the sole in dog poop. She never made fun of me after that.

Wanda purses her lips. "I keep going back and editing the opening lines. I need to let the story flow, but I can't help but edit the beginning. By the time I move on, I've lost the thread, and I get stuck."

Thinking of my experiences when I paint and sculpt, I say, "I'm in visual arts, and I've found the creative process works best if I turn off my internal critic. Maybe you could try writing without stopping for short bursts? That might help."

She nods. "I forgot about that trick, thanks for reminding me. I'll try it. I need to turn off the internet too. All those notifications distract me. Do you want to get a coffee before we talk?"

I sniff the air and inhale the smell of espresso. I prefer the local Fidalgo Coffee for a rich, full flavor. It goes down easy and doesn't call attention to itself. But I don't want to waste time ordering a beverage. I want to get down to business and talk about the missing notebook.

I say, "I'm set. This won't take long, and thanks for taking time to talk."

She gets out a notebook and pen, poised to take notes. Whose story is this? Mine, or hers, or the whole town's?

"My dad told me the journal is missing," she says. "But

are you sure someone took it? Maybe it's in the trash out back. Or, it might be somewhere tucked away in your café? Have you searched everywhere inside?"

Screwing up my face, I scold myself. I suspected people of stealing it, but I didn't stop to consider that it might have been tossed out with the trash. When I get home, I'll dig through the dumpster.

Sweat trickles down my arms. If Gigi was here, she'd give me a talking to for jumping to conclusions. These are my neighbors, not my adversaries.

"You have a point," I say. "For some reason, I got it into my head that the diary was stolen. A lot of people were in the café at the time. Boots told me you asked about it. I have to cover all bases, and I need to ask, did you take the journal by mistake? Maybe tuck it into your purse? I'd understand it if you did because you're writing a novel. I wouldn't tell anyone you had it if you give it back to me."

She sits back and stares. "I don't need to read the journal to write a story about it. Inspiration comes to me unbidden. Creativity flows, and I listen to the characters. I don't have to lift from someone's life. I'm not a fiction vampire who mines lives for stories."

I am quiet and mull over what to say next. In writing about the journal, she is basing her story on my life. A surge of artistic jealousy courses through me. She's in Starbuck's writing, while I had to jettison my passion for art and leave it back in Seattle.

I sigh. One day, I'd like to hire a reliable helper in the

café. They'd cook food and serve it. I'd set up my potter's wheel in the basement. The feeling of slick, wet clay beneath my fingertips calms me. The wheel goes round, and the motor drones. When I push on the foot pedal for more speed, a vase or bowl grows under my hands. It's magic, and I miss it.

She says, "You were saying?"

Lacing my fingers together, I say, "I'm sorry. I didn't mean to offend you. I might be a little bit jealous of you. You have the freedom to write all day, while I work at the restaurant."

Wanda's eyes open wide. "You're jealous? I sit on my butt trying to crank out one thousand beautiful words each day, and I fall flat on my face, despite my education. You, on the other hand, make gorgeous pottery. I've seen it. Gigi showed it to me. You have a gift. And your grandmother loved you. Anyone could've seen that. I wanted her to be my grandmother."

My shoulders relax. "Thank you for saying that about my art and my grandmother. I feel like a squirrel hunting for acorns at Gigi's, running around and responding to requests. It is the opposite of working alone creating art."

"Try meditating," she says. "Take a moment to yourself before you open. Set boundaries. My dad does at his store, or he'd be wrung out when he got home. And don't give up on your art. Keep going. Find a few hours on your days off."

I smile. We're more alike than I thought. "I'll give it a

shot. You know, we could be art accountability buddies. You'll tell me how the writing is going, and if you turned off the distractions and wrote for however many minutes is your goal. I'll report in about centering myself before guests arrive in the morning to set the tone of the day, and about whether I've sketched, or painted, or worked in clay on a day off."

She extends a hand. "Deal."

We grin at each other and shake. Her grip is strong.

She says, "I think I'm going to like this. All right, so, back to the diary. Where were we before we got off topic?"

"I'm trying to uncover every possibility. I want it back in my house and in my hands. I don't want anyone else to read it before I do. Do you have any idea where it might be?"

She looks up at the ceiling, as if gathering ideas. "I have no idea. It could be so many people. My best bet is your cousin. The one in high school who rolls her eyes a lot?"

"But Lydia wasn't there when the diary disappeared."

Wanda shakes her head. "I saw her when I went in the restroom. She was in the kitchen texting. She could've taken it to remember your grandmother by, as a keepsake." She jabs at finger at me. "And she wouldn't tell you because she wants it all to herself. She probably hid it under the mattress in her bedroom."

She sits back and beams, as if satisfied with her story.

I nod. I can see Lydia taking it and not telling me. Growing up, I sensed she was jealous of the attention Gigi gave me. I'll have to find a way to check Lydia's room or just plain ask her if she has it.

"Thanks, that's helpful. I didn't know Lydia was there. But did you happen to see a man wearing a newsboy cap and a green raincoat with a hood?"

"Nope, I didn't see him. But I like the newsboy cap detail. I'll use it in my story. By the way, Mr. Frackus came by as we were leaving. He picked something up off the sidewalk. Do you think someone dropped the diary, and he has it?"

"I'm not sure. But it could be anyone at this point. I'm going to get to the bottom of it and recover my grand-mother's journal no matter what it takes. Except for breaking the law, that is."

As I leave, I say to the gray-haired woman reading by the window, "Thanks for watching my bike."

"I didn't look out. I'm getting to a good part in my book." Ms. Tinsley puts down her book. "I know you from the high school. But you didn't have that business in your nose back then, did you? But you did something that caused a ruckus. Let's see if I can remember what it was." She taps her chin.

I gulp. I'll never escape being known as the one who threw a water balloon that hit the principal during the Fourth of July parade. After the miniature donkeys went by, there was a gap in the procession. I aimed for my friend Regina on the other side of the street.

Just as I arced the green water balloon, which I'd filled at home without Gigi's knowledge, into the air, a Cadillac convertible went by. The shot fell short with a splat.

The parade stopped mid-beat. Everyone stared at me. Water dripped down Mr. Harding's flushed face. I stood there slack-jawed and frozen.

He pointed a finger at me. "She did it."

I turned and ran home. When Gigi heard about it, which she did minutes later, she reamed me out. I had to clean classrooms with Midge, the janitor, for a week that summer before tenth grade as punishment. Regina distanced herself from me, and I became a loner. One water balloon sealed my fate.

I nod now and brace for a scolding. I say, "I just moved back from Seattle."

"I hear you're doing a marvelous job managing your grandmother's café. That must be a huge undertaking. Good for you. I applaud your courage to take it on, and your allegiance to Gigi's memory. Not many people your age would carry on the family business. They want to flitter and flutter about, doing techy things." She glares. "Or not work and laze around all day playing video games."

I give her a smile. "Thanks for the compliment. Be sure to stop in sometime."

"I will. I like a strong cup of coffee with my scone."

I say goodbye, wave to Wanda, who doesn't notice, and get back on my bike.

There are too many suspects. I need to start a spreadsheet and write them down. And I must speak with Mr. Frackus. Did he know my grandmother? Was that why his number was circled in the phone book?

12

That evening, I open my laptop on the kitchen table. This is the room where I feel closest to my grandmother. I jot down the names of people who might have the journal. The man with the green raincoat and newsboy cap. Mr. Frackus, my high school science teacher. Boots Brinker, her brother Guns, and her father. Kenny Robinson and Wanda, the writer, Ellie, and little Maddie who wants to help me find it. Shane and Lydia are suspects. I doubt Bets and Zerk have it, but I add their names. I have the feeling they were sincere when they whispered about retiring from a life of crime.

There were other guests in the cafe yesterday afternoon, but I can't remember who they were. It's a blur. Serve scones, pick up plates, pour more coffee. Heat quiche in the microwave. Scoop blackberry jam from a Mason jar. Hustle into the café, set the items down and repeat the process, over and over. Whew.

I tap a pen on the edge of the table and try to come up with other suspects. I need a side kick who will help me brainstorm ideas. With a partner, I'd do a more thorough job.

I type up the list and pause. Mike, the boater, might've been there. I add his name.

Getting up, I pace the kitchen floor. The list is long. I hold up my hands. Who am I kidding? I'm not a detective. I'm an artist and not even an amateur sleuth. I need help, and I have no one to turn to.

My phone rings. I don't recognize the number, but I answer it. I've given out business cards, so it could be someone calling with a tip.

"This is Karina," I say, hoping the caller will say they have the red diary.

"This is Mr. Frackus. I'm returning your call." His voice is as deep as the Grand Canyon. Gigi took me there a few years after my folks died. She said we deserved a road trip, with lots of ice cream along the way. I was all for that idea.

I stop in my tracks. "Thank you for calling me back. I've run into a bit of a situation and wondered if you had time to talk."

"Sure. What's the problem? Is the mixer on the blink again?"

I cock my head. Why is he talking about the mixer? "No, it's not the mixer. I'm looking for my grandmother's journal. It went missing yesterday around the time a few people said you were walking by. I heard you picked something off the sidewalk out front. Did you happen to pick up a notebook with a red leather cover?"

"I did go by yesterday afternoon. But I don't have the item you described."

I sigh. If Mr. Frackus had it, my search would've ended, easy-peasy, as Gigi liked to say. Instead, I now need to interview each person.

"Did you see anything suspicious?" I say. "Like someone hurrying outside or slipping something in their pocket?"

"No, I didn't."

"Thanks. Well, it's late. I guess I'll give up on the search tonight."

"Good luck," he says.

Hanging up, I wonder again about his remark about the mixer. Did Mr. Frackus happen to know my grandmother? She didn't mention him in my presence. Was he in the kitchen, helping her, and I didn't know it?

I shake my head and lock the doors, heading up to bed. My mind is swimming with suspects.

I draw a bath and dip my toe in. The temperature is just right. Setting a blue towel on the floor, I climb in and let my cares drift away.

Soaking in warm water, knots in my neck relax. My favorite activity growing up was taking a bubble bath in the white porcelain claw foot tub. Gigi and I loved our baths.

My phone rings downstairs, and I debate what to do.

Do I stay in the bath, or run downstairs and possibly receive important information?

Grabbing a towel, I get out.

Water sloshes in the tub as I pull on my terrycloth bathrobe and head down the stairs.

By the time I get there, the ringing stops. I don't recognize the number. I check for voice mail, but the caller didn't leave a message.

Wind whistles through a gap in the windows.

A branch skitters across the roof.

My eyebrows shoot up. I tense and stop to listen, alone in a creaking old house.

I rub my arms and hurry into the kitchen, leaving bare footprints on the floor. I slap together a honey sandwich and take it upstairs to eat in the bath. But when I step into the tub, the water is lukewarm.

I say, "So, this is how it is going to be? A struggle all the way, everyday?"

I pull out the white rubber stopper and drain the tub.

"The missing notebook," I say, pulling on pajamas in my bedroom. "The broken-down car? Shane dating Lydia and her about to quit on me? But don't worry, I can handle it. I'm just another struggling, suffering artist. Nothing to stare at on this roadside. No news here, move along."

I crawl into bed and sit up against the brass bedframe, reading a book while I eat with the plate propped on my stomach.

Someone knocks on the kitchen door, rapping hard three times.

I jerk and yelp. The porcelain plate flies down to the floor, crashing and breaking into jagged pieces.

Cussing, I hop out of bed on the other side and slip on my bathrobe. I bend down and pull my baseball bat out from under the bed.

"We're closed," I yell.

The knocking continues.

Good grief. It's late. What is this person thinking?

Lydia and Shane stand at the back door.

When I open it, she comes in and flaps her arms.

"We were out there forever. Did you forget we're coming over?"

Shane glances at me with a slight smile.

"Come in," I say. "And make yourselves at home. Yes, I forgot. I've had a few other things on my mind. Like overseeing a business and finding the diary. And taking a hot bath that turned cold because I answered the phone. And no one left a message."

Lydia rolls her eyes. "No one leaves messages. Voice mail is for oldsters."

"I called," Shane says. "To say we were on our way, so

we wouldn't surprise you, which we clearly did." He motions to the side of my mouth. "You have a little crumb there. Want me to brush it off?"

I frown. I must look like a mess. Licking my lips, I say, "No, I don't need your help. Well, actually I do. Do you guys want to review my list of suspects? You might be able to add some."

"A list of suspects?" Lydia says. "It's just a diary and not that big a deal."

My hands tremble. Not a big deal? What planet is she on?

"It is a big deal, to me, at least," I say. "And if you don't understand that, maybe you shouldn't work here. Gigi was my everything. She was all I had after my parents died." I brush a tear from my eye.

"Don't forget about me and my mom," she says. "We're here for you."

"You are. And even though you're nearby, I feel alone at times, rattling around in this big, old place. I want her diary in my hands, and then I'll feel like she's here with me."

I grab a tissue from a box and blow my nose.

Shane pats my arm. "You're going through a tough time. We'll help, won't we Lyds?"

"But we were going to watch a movie tonight," she says. "I was looking forward to it."

"We can do that another time," he says, putting an arm around her shoulder.

She leans into him. "Okay, let's help Karina."

An hour later, the kitchen smells of popcorn. A stain-less-steel bowl rests on the counter with only kernels remaining.

Glancing across the table at the lovebirds, who are eying each other, I say, "I think we should wrap it up. We haven't made any progress, except consumed large amounts of popcorn."

Lydia says, "And beer for you and Shane, which you wouldn't let me have."

Shaking my head, I'm reminded of their age differ-ence. Why is he dating her? Was he desperate and couldn't find someone his own age?

"Are you going to bed already?" Lydia says. "You can watch a movie with us."

I've kept her at a distance and been wrapped up in myself after returning home. It wouldn't hurt me to sit on the sofa next to them and hang out for one night.

"You know what?" I say. "That sounds good, watching a movie. The house has been making weird noises that spook me at night. I could use some company."

"Great," she says, her eyes lighting up.

Shane says, "Sounds good."

I open a closet and take out a pile of quilts.

"Hold on for a few minutes," I say. "I broke a plate and need to clean it up. This won't take long."

I race upstairs with a dust pan and broom, sweeping up porcelain shards. I use the vacuum to remove fragments. They clink and clatter in the long plastic black hose.

Trotting downstairs, I join them. Soon, we're watching a new movie on Netflix and laughing together. Pulling a quilt up to my chin, I smile. This is much better than eating alone in bed.

13

The café is closed on Sundays and Mondays, because Gigi said she needed two days off or her ankles would swell up like balloons. But there is much to be done to prepare for when we open again. I roll out quiche crusts in the kitchen on Sunday morning. Music plays in the background, coming from my phone. A song comes on about writing in a diary, and I frown. Where is Gigi's journal? And what was Violet about to say to me when I saw her at the pub, before her team came in? When I have time, I'll text her to meet up.

I place crusts in round baking pans and crimp the edges, pricking dough on the bottom with a fork, so it won't puff up. Sliding the pans into the oven, I set an alarm on my phone and turn off the music.

It's time to keep my promise to Wanda, my new art friend, to meditate early each day. As in any relationship with another creative person, I'm awed at her accomplishments and jealous of her at the same time. She has the freedom to sit and write all day. But I shouldn't make assumptions. I'm not familiar with her financial situation. For all I know, she might have three months to write a novel before going out and getting a job.

I sit on the floor and lean back against the kitchen cabinet, folding my legs in a crisscross applesauce pose I learned in kindergarten. I breathe in slowly, hold it, and let it out.

I picture myself being calm. I'm in a grassy field, running with open arms. Everything is easy. I'm smiling. I'm laughing. I have the journal in my hands. My cares and worries are gone.

Someone knocks on the back door.

My pulse races. I jump up and hurry to the locked door, looking out.. No one's going to breeze in and take anything else of Gigi's while I'm in charge.

Jeff, my former boyfriend from Seattle, is at the door. He cups his hands to see in. He's tall and looks like a Great Blue Heron, hunched over.

I cock my head, wondering why he is here. I broke up with him before returning to Millersville to help Gigi. He was busy with his band, rehearsing and playing gigs, practicing on his drum set in the living room. In our daily lives, we rarely saw each other.

When I got the call from Aunt Jean about my grandmother, something clicked inside. I knew it was time to end my relationship with Jeff. When I told him, he shrugged, and then we divided up our possessions. I got the red oven mitt we bought at a garage sale. Oh joy.

Opening the door, I say, "Hey, come on in. This is quite the surprise."

He strides in with a lanky glide. "Thought I'd stop by. Haven't heard from you."

My phone dings. The quiche crusts are ready to come out of the oven.

"Sit down," I say, "and make yourself at home. I'll take these out of the oven before they burn."

His beard is combed, and he's wearing a new red flannel shirt. He made an effort with his appearance, which is rare. I wonder why he is here and if he wants something from me.

He slides into a seat and drums on the edge of the table. His hands are always in motion. His toes tap out a beat only he can hear.

He says, "So, how is it going? Managing a café sounds like a lot of work."

"It is." I open the oven, and hot air rushes out, blasting me in the face. I pull out the pie plates and set them on metal cooling racks on the counter. I close the oven door.

"Twenty-four-seven is an understatement," I say. "It's not all sunshine and roses, like some people might think."

"Neither is making music," he says, leaning back. The chair creaks.

Tension hangs thick in the room. Much is unsaid

between us, given how I left him. This is awkward. I have things to do, and I wish he wasn't here. But I want to hear what he has to say about our friends.

"Coffee?" I say.

"Please, the two-hour drive was three hours. Nasty traffic all the way north."

I pour two scoops of coffee beans into the grinder. Before closing the jar holding the beans, I dip my nose in and inhale a rich, nutty aroma. The smell reminds me of my grandmother and brings me back to center. I'm home.

I say, "I haven't been back to Seattle. I've been too busy."

I push on the coffee grinder. The machine whirs, blocking out conversation and allowing me to consider why Jeff showed up. I hope he doesn't want to get back together. If and when I decide to date again, I'll pick someone else. We've had our run.

I push the button to start the coffee maker and sit down. Like Gigi, I am content with a straight-forward brew for my favorite beverage. I don't crave fancy coffee shop drinks, which is fortunate given my tight financial situation. My student loan is hanging over me like a dark cloud about to burst and shower me with cold rain.

"Have you had time to throw any pots?" he says. "Or paint?"

He tips the chair back and holds eye contact

I shake my head. "Not yet. I haven't had time, but I will."

"I know that's important to you." He smiles, "It makes you happy. Don't let the café consume you. Make time to be creative, like I do."

I sigh. If only he knew how much work running the café involves. My grandmother deserves a Wonder Woman award. She never complained.

Before the coffee maker beeps, I get up and pour two cups from the carafe. It would taste better if I waited, but I want to get this over with and get on with my day. I set two cups of coffee down and add cream, sugar, and a spoon for him.

I put my elbows on the table. "It's good to see you, but why did you come?"

He leans forward. "I was talking with a new friend of mine, Ned. She's a reporter. She said there's a rumor going around that you have a map that leads to buried treasure. She's on her way here to check out the story."

I cross my arms. Jeff is someone who is out for himself, searching for something that will make him whole. He craves fame and refuses to work odd jobs. He says they are beneath him. I was the one who paid the rent by temping in offices three days a week. Before I broke it off, I realized he expected me to pay his way forever. He wanted to play his drums all day while I paid the bills.

I sit back and say, "I know Ned. She was in town when the riots broke out. But why would she care about a treasure map? She covers breaking news."

He taps on the table. "You'll have to ask her. But I think this is big. Let me in on it. We could get rich."

I shake my head. There is no us, and the missing object is mine. But I won't tell him about the details. If he heard the story about the stock market crash and that my grandmother hid money, he'd hound me and want to horn in on the money Gigi left. Because that's his style. I let out a weary sigh. I'm tired from working long hours and getting little sleep. I don't want to deal with Jeff right now.

"Listen," I say to set him straight, "small town gossip has blown things out of proportion. Rumors are flying. The fact is, my grandmother's journal is gone, and it only is important to me. Let's forget about it. How're you doing?"

He scratches his chin. "Are you sure? You wouldn't be holding out on me, would you? So, you get first chance at a hidden pot of gold?"

I roll my eyes. "Like that's going to happen. So, have you seen any of our friends?"

"Yep. Lynne is showing her photography in an exhibit in Pioneer Square. Rusty is selling terra cotta teapots in New York City. He has an agent."

A pang of envy slices through me. Rusty has an agent, and I don't. I left what I love behind, which is creating art. Everyone is pursuing their craft and moving on without me.

"Say hi to them from me."

"Ron got a gig playing in the ballet orchestra. It's part-time, but he's making ends meet by teaching tuba."

"That's good."

Fifteen minutes later, I get up and usher him to the back door.

"Good to see you," I say. "Take care."

"Hey, wait, I assumed I'd spend the night with you. I brought my stuff."

My mouth drops open. If I let him sleep over, he'll become a permanent guest. I started my life over for Gigi's sake, and I don't need to revisit my relationship with Jeff. That clay pot has been fired in the kiln and won't be shaped or molded into a new form.

I gesture out the door. "Sorry, but no way that's going to happen."

He steps outside. "I could couch-surf for a few nights. But it could turn into more than that, if you want."

I start to close the door. "I'll take what you said as a compliment, but I'll pass. We had our time, and it's gone. I'm starting to like having the creaky old place to myself."

He cocks his head. "Are you seeing someone? Is that why you're turning me down?"

Shaking my head, I say, "That's not why. It's who we were together that isn't right for me, and it is over. I've got to go. Goodbye."

I close the door and lock it.

Putting his hands on the glass, he says, "I told Ned to come see you. I gave her your address."

I groan. Ned already knows where I live and work. She's been in the café in the past. I like her, but I don't need a reporter named Ned nosing around.

My hands clench. I have got to find the diary before someone else does. Apparently word is spreading like wildfire. This town needs more to discuss than my grandmother's private thoughts in a red journal.

I watch as Jeff slinks down the alley, to make sure he's gone, and then go into the kitchen. I recall that Ned is excellent at investigating stories. She records conversations on her phone and writes in a notebook. Perhaps she could help me. I could use her skills to propel the search while she taps me for information.

I shake my head, doubting Ned will show up or call. A tale of a cash hoard told by an old woman who ran the café is not real news. There's no way an editor in Seattle would send a reporter two hours north to cover a strange story about a little town's sudden burst of interest in a missing item. A grandmother's musings is not worth a reporter's time.

I decide to call Mr. Frackus again. He sounded like he was holding something back when we talked. I'm still bothered by why his phone number was circled by my grandmother in the phone book that she insisted on keeping.

A few years back, when we were cleaning out the hall closet, I suggested we recycle the old phone books. But she protested and said she was still using them. I shrugged. We were from different generations, that much was clear.

Now, the White Pages are on the kitchen table, left there when I looked up Mr. Frackus's number. I dial his number, and it rings. I'm about to hang up when he answers.

"Hello?"

"I'm sorry to disturb you, Mr. Frackus. It's Karina again at Gigi's Café."

He clears his throat. "I'm guessing you aren't calling about the grade I gave you senior year?"

I chuckle. "No, I'm not. But I'm still on the hunt for my grandmother's journal. I wanted to ask you, what exactly did you pick up off the sidewalk?"

"I picked up litter."

I tilt my head. Wanda told me he tucked whatever it was in his pocket before hurrying away. No one would do that with litter.

"Are you sure? It would mean so much to me to get the notebook back. I've been asking everyone."

He's quiet for a moment. "Would you like to come over and have a cup of tea? Your grandmother and I used to do that fairly often, after you moved away."

My eyebrows shoot up. I didn't know she kept company with him while I was busy in Seattle. There might be more to my grandmother than I realized.

There are a million other things I should be doing instead of drinking tea, like checking my car battery to see if it needs to be replaced. The mixing bowls on the kitchen counter should be washed. I need to prepare scone dough and chill it. I had planned to set up my potter's wheel in the basement and set my favorite tools out for working in clay. I could sort my sponges by size. But this offer of a visit to learn a new side of my guardian has piqued my curiosity and, of course, it takes priority.

"I'll ride my bike over, because my car won't start. I'll be there in ten or fifteen minutes."

"I'm located at 152 West Elm in a brick rambler with a large front window. You can't miss it. There's a dumpster across the street at my neighbor's house, and they're throwing things out. Good thing you're not driving, because there isn't a place to park."

14

I stop pedaling the bicycle and brake on West Elm. Cars and pickups line the street. Next door to Mr. Frackus's brick rambler, a green dumpster sits in a driveway. Two men in brown coveralls heft a beat-up bathroom vanity out of a house and chuck it into the dumpster.

I turn into my high school teacher's driveway and dismount. Propping the kick stand up, I leave the bike and walk to the door. A million questions flit through my mind. Did my grandmother come here often? Were they friends? Did she invite him home for coffee, a scone, a slice of quiche, and something more?

A shudder runs through me. I never thought of my grandmother as having a romantic side. But perhaps I'm about to find out more.

Mr. Frackus stands at the window with his arms

crossed, glaring at the neighbor's place. Before I can knock, he opens the door.

"Come in, come in. It's quite a mess next door, isn't it? My neighbor is remodeling. It seems like everyone is doing that, except for me. I'm far too thrifty to spend my money upgrading what works perfectly fine for me."

The house smells closed up and sad, like no one has cooked a meal in months. Maybe since my grandmother died.

He says, "I hope you haven't jettisoned what was dear to your grandmother. Don't be too quick to ditch items she surrounded herself with." His upper lip quivers.

"Were you close? It sounds like you were."

He waves the question away. "Come in and sit down. There'll be time to cover that later. Or not."

Wondering what I'll learn, I sit at the dining table while he rummages in the kitchen cupboards. Did my grandmother have a secret lover?

Porcelain clinks. A cup shatters on the tile floor.

"Oh no," he says, sounding upset.

I head into the kitchen to help him.

Bending down, he says in a choked voice, "This was Gigi's favorite. Gone forever. Clumsy, clumsy me."

His hands are full of pottery shards. He straightens up and dumps them in the trash.

My visit might be touching a tender spot for him, if they were good friends. And it is beginning to sound like they were. Come to think of it, Mr. Frackus attended my grandmother's memorial service. He blew his nose into a white handkerchief and honked so loud that I almost didn't hear the minister's final words.

I pat his shoulder. "I'll get a broom and help. I can see this is rattling you. I miss her too."

While I sweep up the remaining broken bits, he brews a pot of tea.

"English Breakfast," he says. "Your grandmother's favorite."

Tapping my lips, I wonder why she never mentioned her visits with him to me, or told me she liked a certain type of tea. I'd thought we were united as coffee drinkers. But apparently she was sipping tea behind my back.

"I'll take the teapot to the table," I say.

I set it down in a dim dining room. The walls are yellowed. It looks like the original paint color was once white. Heavy drapes cover a window. This is a place of sadness, where grief permeates the rooms.

My throat grows tight with tears. I miss her, but wallowing won't bring her back. I go back to the kitchen to check on him.

He says, "I'm warming the cups. Your grandmother insisted we do that."

I raise an eyebrow. We? If he's telling the truth, why didn't Gigi mention him? For a moment, I wonder if his memories are false. He could have harbored a one-sided crush. Everyone loved my grandmother, and he is one of many who miss her.

When we sit down, he sets a plate of gingersnaps between us. Everyone is serving me cookies with ginger. Is it a new trend? If so, I didn't get the text.

He tugs on an earlobe. "My fondness for Gigi must come as a surprise to you."

I press my lips together and nod, not sure what to say. I'm here to listen and gather information.

"We started going out before you graduated from high school." He smiles. "We were sneaking around like teenagers. She wouldn't spend the night or let me tell anyone we were sweet on each other. At first, it was because I was your teacher. She didn't want it to affect my relationship with you. But I suspected she was holding back part of her heart."

He pulls out a white handkerchief and dabs at his eyes.

"When you moved to Seattle, we grew closer and saw more of each other. I retired and had time on my hands. I worked in Gigi's yard, to keep it spiffed up for customers."

Blowing out a breath, I realize there is more to my grandmother than I ever knew or could have imagined. I sip tea and take comfort in the warm liquid sliding down my throat. My world has shifted. What I thought was true, that my guardian was a widow with no regrets, was a trick. It comes as a relief to know my grandmother had a love life. She gave others so much. She deserved to have a special friendship.

"Go on," I say. "This is interesting. I had no idea."

"Your grandmother was a private person, and she doted on you. She said because you lost both parents at a young age, she wanted to give you twice as much. You came first."

Tears stream down my cheeks. I wait for what he will say next.

He sighs. "She wouldn't let me help her in the kitchen, by baking or washing dishes. She said it was her domain and only you or Lydia were welcome in the back of the house."

His hands quiver as he lifts a cup to his mouth. He slurps and sets it down.

"When the café was closed, we'd walk on the beach, holding hands. We'd have picnics in her back yard. We'd spread out a blanket and pretend we were in high school." He utters a choked laugh.

"The hardest thing about missing your grandmother is that very few people in town knew we were in love. It was the best kept secret in Millersville."

I nod. It is near impossible in our town to keep a lid on a new love. Everyone watches and smiles, gossiping with neighbors about what is nobody's business.

His eyes brim with tears. "She wrote me letters and mailed them from the post office. I'd get them the next day, or if a carrier was new, a few days later. Would you like to see one?"

I say, "Yes, I would. It sounds like something she'd do,

mail a letter across town. I'd love to read part of one she wrote."

He gets up and goes to the coffee table in the living room. Picking up a large book, he brings it over to the dining table. He opens it to an envelope stuck between two pages. It's addressed to him in my grandmother's flowery cursive handwriting. The return address says: Gigi's.

"We admired Ansel Adams's photographs, so that's why I kept her letters tucked in this book. Before her death, she took most of them back and burned them. She didn't want you to read them. But it's okay if you read the one here. She asked me to save it for you."

He hands me a white envelope.

I take it with shaking hands. I didn't expect to discover a secret love affair. The paper smells of lavender and Gigi, despite being stored in a book and having been shunted through the postal system.

"Go ahead and open it," he says, patting the table.

I pull out the letter and smooth the paper on the table top.

Reading Gigi's words, I hear her voice, as if she's speaking to me.

"Dear Karina, by now you must have realized I had a long, fond friendship with Mr. Bernard Frackus. I'm sorry to have hidden it from you, but I thought you weren't ready to share me, even though you were old enough to leave town, and you came home for visits. It's my doing too. I wanted what you and I had to be special. My mission was for us to be so close that you wouldn't have a chance to miss your parents. Of course, that wasn't possible. But it was my aspiration."

My tears fall on the page. Gigi, why didn't you tell me? I would've been fine with you loving someone else. You didn't have to keep this a secret. I wanted you to be happy.

"Most of all, I want you to know that I love you beyond words. Beyond the moon and the stars and all the scones in the universe, you are my special Kit Kat. And thank you for taking over my café. And now I need to tell you one last thing about your parents."

I turn the paper over, but it's blank. "Where's the next page?"

"That's the last letter I got from her, and it's exactly how it came."

I clear my throat. She is gone. It is too late to ask her what she meant. Did she forget to include the next page?

"I want to read the rest," I say. "Do you know what she meant to say? What did she mean about my parents?"

He shakes his head. "She wouldn't tell me. She said it was too big to share even with me. Too risky if it got out."

My stomach clenches, and my mind churns with ideas. Was she going to tell me something about how my parents died? Did they cause the accident? Was my mother pregnant, and the medical examiner discovered that? Did I have a little baby brother or sister I never knew about? What if the child was born while my mother was dying, and the baby was adopted? And no one told me?

I rub my temples. A million possibilities are running through my mind, giving me a splitting headache. I sniff and swallow my tears.

Mr. Frackus hands me a tissue.

I blow my nose and lean back in the chair. "This is a lot to take in."

Mr. Frackus pulls out a piece of paper. "There's more. I know what your grandmother's handwriting looks like. And that's why I picked this off the sidewalk outside the café yesterday afternoon. I knew it was hers."

He holds up a page that is torn along the edge.

I take it from him and examine it. "It looks like it's been ripped out of a notebook. And this is her writing, you're right."

He shrugs. "I was keeping it for sentimental reasons. But you can have it. I hope it'll help you find her journal."

15

I face Mr. Frackus and pull together the facts. A page from Gigi's journal was left in front of the café on Friday. Mr. Frackus picked it up. He goes by every day on his afternoon walk, and I wave to him when I see him.

I rub my eyes and study the writing. It looks like a grocery shopping list. Eggs, butter, flour, milk, and cream. But at the bottom in tiny writing are words that make my stomach drop. "Sit Karina down and tell her about her sibling. Tell her the truth and get it over with. She is old enough to understand. I can't let her find out from someone else. She'd never forgive me."

My jaw drops. "I don't understand. What did she mean by this? She never told me about a brother or sister. Was she confused when she wrote this?"

He wipes his brow. "I have no idea. Certain things she

kept from me. But she did say she had some secrets to share with you. That's all I know. I guess she never got around to it."

I frown and flop back in the chair, crossing my arms. "This comes as a complete surprise. I thought we were honest with each other. And now I find out she died with secrets." I wave my hands for emphasis. "All that time, she hid how she cared for you from me. I would've welcomed knowing she had love in her life."

I glare at the ripped page before me. My hands clench with frustration. I can't get her to explain. All her answers went with her. Nevermore can I ask for Gigi's insights.

My pulse throbs in my temples. I'm surprised the paper doesn't burst into flames from my scorching stare. Why didn't she share her secrets with me? I've always wanted a sibling. She knew that. I would have embraced the news. For the first time in my life, I feel that Gigi let me down.

I bite my lower lip. Is my sibling alive? Were they adopted out? Where do they live? Having a sister or a brother would be fabulous. My mind spins with possibilities.

Blowing out a breath, I say, "There is a lot we don't know. And I don't have the faintest idea where to start. But let's begin with this one page you found. And thank you for giving it to me."

He nods. "You're welcome. I understand this is a difficult time for you, with Gigi gone, and the journal missing, and now your reading about a sibling you didn't know you had. I do wish she had spoken with you about it. But maybe we'll never know the truth."

I tap the table with my fist. "I'll find out, no matter what it takes. I've got to know if I have a brother or a sister. Maybe I have a crop of siblings I don't know about." I shake my head. "If only she'd been honest with me. Why was she afraid to tell me? That doesn't sound like the grandmother I grew up with."

He rubs his chin. "She told me she thought the news might devastate you. Apparently your parents weren't who you thought they were."

I grip the table edge. "How could they not be who I thought they were? This is utterly frustrating and confusing. I'm left without answers, and it's making me angry at her."

"I share your confusion, and I wish I could give you answers. I'm just repeating what she told me."

I move the paper around on the table, making a circle. I'm light-headed from hearing all this. I wish I could sit down with Gigi and question her. But I must move on and find answers on my own.

I say, "Let's start with this torn out piece of paper. Who ripped it out and tossed it on the ground? Why pull this page out from all the rest?"

Mr. Frackus holds up his hands. "I have no idea. But given what it says, I'm glad I picked it up and took it with me. We don't want gossip getting started."

A shudder runs through me, thinking of how the rumor mill would spread this private, most personal information like wildfire. I turn the page over and read more of my grandmother's handwriting.

"What you seek, you will find under a cloth protecting the surface which holds my hair. I've tucked the clue away from prying eyes, dear. This is for you."

I say, "What do you think she meant by that? Is this some kind of riddle?"

He touches the frames of his glasses. "Possibly, yes. But I'm not sure."

I nod. When I was ten, she'd hide clues around the house and time how long it took for me to find the last one. It would be hidden in a sock, or wrapped around a chocolate bar, or behind a stack of folded, clean dish towels.

"Eureka," I'd yell, jumping up and down. "I found it."

"She did like to be mysterious," I say.

"I bet you'll solve the riddle. Let it simmer in the back of your mind and don't dwell on it. It'll come to you when you're not focused on it."

We sit in silence for a few beats. My mind is blank. Adding a mystery about a possible new family member is almost too much for my brain. If I was an electric mixer, I'd have shorted out by now.

"Take the page with you," he says, "and the envelope and the letter. I hope you'll find answers about your potential sibling when you recover Gigi's journal. By the way, I'd like to read the diary when you get it back. It would be like visiting with her and holding her in my arms again."

He coughs and blinks, looking down and picking a piece of lint off his gray pants.

My face heats. I erase an image of the two of them being intimate and blow out a breath. This day is getting stranger and stranger. My grandmother and my high school science teacher were a couple? And I didn't suspect a thing. Gigi must have worked hard to keep it a secret.

He says, "You said your car is giving you troubles? I might be able to fix it."

I break into a smile. "That'd be great. It might be the battery, but I'm not sure. I haven't checked it yet."

He stands. "We'll put the bike in my trunk and go over to Gigi's. I'll take a look."

Springing out of my seat, I'm glad to have a task to focus on, instead of missing Gigi with all my heart and wondering what she meant to say to me. And why, oh why, did she write about her hair? I doubt I'll ever answer that question.

We wrestle the bike into the car. The handlebars stick out, so we don't close the trunk. It's odd to work in tandem with my teacher, who turned out to be my grandmother's secret lover. I'll have to sleep on this mind-blowing revelation to get used to the idea. I suspect it will take months to wrap my mind around it.

At my house, Mr. Frackus opens the hood of my car and checks the battery.

"It's dead," he says. "I've got a trickle charger. I can hook it up."

"Perfect. Let's do that."

"It will take a while to charge though. If you need to go somewhere soon, I can give you a jump start."

He's handy, helpful, and pleasant, so I almost understand why my grandmother fell for him. But I feel bad that I missed out on sharing a major part of her inner life. How can a blood relative living in the same house not know their guardian is seeing someone on the sly? Maybe I didn't want to see it.

I say, "I have to go make scones, so I'm not in a hurry. I'll be fine waiting."

"Did you leave the overhead light on, or the door ajar? That'll drain your battery."

I nod. "I might have. I've been distracted since Gigi died and blaming myself about the diary going missing. Do you have any idea what she meant about a cloth protecting the surface which holds her hair?"

He shrugs. "Beats me. I can't help you there, only with your car."

I purse my lips, nursing a burning desire to solve the mystery of the missing journal. I am driven by a hunger to learn if I have a sister or brother, and if the person is alive, and where they live, and what they're like.

I cringe. What if I dislike my sibling and can't stand

them after going to the trouble of uncovering their iden-tity and tracking them down? What will I do then?

Glancing at Mr. Frackus, I nod and decide if Gigi trusted him, I can too. He was a science teacher, and he is fascinated with facts. He might spot something I over-looked. With his help, we could figure the puzzle out together.

I say, "I could use your assistance in looking for clues. Why don't you come in, and we'll comb through the house? With two of us looking, we'll have a better chance of deciphering what Gigi meant."

He glances at the back door. "She wouldn't have wanted me to meddle."

"I bet she'd want you to help me. That must be why she left a letter for me at your place, and not here. She could have given it to me. Or had the hospice worker put it on the kitchen counter. She meant for us to work as a team, and she wanted me to learn that you were a couple. She must've really cared for you. Will you help me? Please, say yes?"

His eyes light up, as if he hasn't been needed or had this much fun in a long time.

"Yes, I will. I'll definitely do that. It'll bring back fond memories of your grandmother."

Guiding him inside, we go room by room and come up empty handed.

We stop at the threshold to her bedroom. He stands with his hands hanging at his sides. His eyes are moist.

I pause before going in. It feels disrespectful to sort through her things, but that's what we're about to do. I had wanted to leave her room untouched. But her tantalizing mention about the hair has changed my mind.

I step inside, as if my grandmother invited me, and motion for him to follow. Which she did, in a cryptic way, through her partial letter.

His voice cracks when he says, "I've always wanted to stay overnight in this room."

I put a hand on top of the dresser to steady myself. An image flashes before me of my science teacher and grandmother in the same bed. I shake it away.

"Let's get this over with," I say.

He looks in the closet, while I open a drawer in the oak dresser.

I doubt she would want him seeing her bras and panties, so I block his view of the contents with my body. But what do I know, maybe she acted different around him and paraded her ample breasts with pride. There is so much about my grandmother I didn't know. She has become a woman of mystery beyond the grave.

I run a hand along the bottom of the drawer. Nothing is hidden under the lingerie, so I slide it shut and open the next one. It's full of socks and a sewing kit with a wooden darning egg decorated with a drawing of a windmill. Maybe this is a souvenir from a trip before I came along. I've never seen it before.

Feeling under the socks, I pull out a scrap of paper and say, "Found something."

"What is it?"

He comes over, and we read a fortune: 'You will have a rich, full life.'

He smiles. "We went to the Lucky Chopsticks on our first date. That's when she got that fortune. I didn't know she kept it."

He glances in the drawer. "And I gave her that darning egg. I got it when I took a trip to Holland, Michigan."

"Did my grandmother go with you?"

"She was too busy taking care of the café. She was waiting for you to come home, so she could take time off. It was wearing her out. I told her to close the café, but she refused. She wanted to leave the cafe for you to take over, so you'd have a home to return to filled with happy memories. In this house, she said, you'd never be without her."

Folding my arms, I'm racked with guilt. It never occurred to me that keeping Gigi's open was a burden for my grandmother. She was worn out, but I was carefree in Seattle. She had foregone holidays because I was too inconsiderate to offer to step in and give her a break.

Instead, I'd driven to California, Oregon, and British Columbia. I'd hiked by the ocean as surf pounded and walked in old growth forests at the base of mighty mountains. And she had been at home, working. I hang my head at how selfish I was.

My muscles tense, and my hands fist. I could run five miles fast to vent my frustration with my worst enemy, which is myself. Why wasn't I kinder to her? Why didn't I give more of myself to help her and step up as an adult?

"It opens," he says, twisting the darning egg. It comes apart. "Hello, what's this?"

I stop thinking about myself and snap to, paying attention.

He peers through his black-rimmed glasses and plucks out a coin. "It's a dime."

"It must have sentimental attachment?" I say. "I don't think this is what she meant by hiding the money she took out of the bank."

He chuckles and examines the coin. "It was minted in her birth year. Must be why she kept it."

I say, "I think we need to focus on finding the diary and not be distracted by a dime."

"You're right," he says, setting it down.

I tuck the darning egg into the drawer and look around the room. A cloth on top of the dresser catches my attention. Her hairbrush rests on it.

Setting the hairbrush aside, I pull back the cloth and expose a folded, cream-colored piece of paper.

My pulse picks up. "I found something."

16

I hold my breath and clutch the note. Gigi hid this under her hairbrush. She wanted me to find it. In a tight voice, I say, "It was under a cloth on the dresser, hidden under her hairbrush. Just like she said it would be."

Mr. Frackus grins. "Gigi would be proud of you. Go ahead and open it. See what it says."

My hands tremble. Opening the folded page, I read four words. "Follow the first left."

I hand it to him.

He says, "But what does that mean?" He runs a hand through his salt and pepper hair. "This is very confusing. It doesn't clear things up, not at all."

I swallow hard. "I miss her and wish she was here, so we could ask her."

"I do too. I've thought that many times."

"I miss her like the Milky Way," I say. "She's far away, but I can still see her."

He says in a choked voice, "She was my Saturn. I was a moon circling her, and I'll be that way forever."

We are quiet. The house creaks. A branch scratches at the window pane.

"I hope when we find the journal," I say, "we'll understand what she meant. But she was hallucinating at times in the months before she died. She said it was from the pain meds. This could be an imaginary game where there aren't any answers."

I frown. The games Gigi and I played when I was a child involved searching for a box of Junior Mints or a bag of gummy bears tucked between two towels in the linen closet. Finding them was a victory prize and kept me looking for an hour. But now the stakes are much higher.

An idea occurs to me, and I say, "Let's go look in the linen closet. It is in the hall and on the left. I have a hunch she may have hidden something there."

Leaving the stale air of the closed-up bedroom behind, we step into the hall and turn left.

I open the linen closet and slip my hands between sheets and towels, groping around. When I pull out a set of crisp, ironed sheets, something falls out and drops to the floor. It rolls. It's a nesting doll about six inches high and painted in red, black, and gold.

I bend and scoop it up in my hands. My heart thumps as I pull off the top. Inside is a tiny silver charm that is shaped like a shovel. She wore it on a chain around her neck.

I say in a soft voice, "She remembered. I always wanted to have this, and I wondered where it was after she died."

I wipe away tears with the back of my hand. "The charm is a reminder of her, but I'd rather have my grandmother. I guess we don't get to pick who sticks around."

He honks into a handkerchief. "No, we don't."

I blow my nose and say, "Let's go downstairs. I could use a cup of coffee. How about you?"

"That's a good idea. The best yet. Your grandmother made wonderful coffee."

I nod as we go down to the country-style kitchen. "Go ahead and sit. I'll get it for you."

Fifteen minutes later, we hunker down across the table holding steaming mugs of coffee. We review the list of suspects and discuss who might have the journal.

I set down my cup. "It seems like everyone has a motive to take it. Wanda is writing a novel about the diary. Boots wants to use it for research for an economics paper. Guns looked interested. Bob Brinker wanted to look at it. Lydia might have taken it for a keepsake. Aunt Jean might want it because it was her mother's. Kenny Robinson is a history buff who'd like to peruse the pages. Maddie and Ellie Robinson sounded like they'd like to examine it. Shane was in the shop when it disappeared, and so was the man in a green raincoat who was wearing a newsboy cap."

Mr. Frackus says, "That is quite a long list you have."

I hold up an index finger. "That's not all. Mr. Rasmus, the librarian, would like to read it. And my ex-boyfriend, Jeff, from Seattle stopped by. He wants to find it. He heard it contains clues to find hidden money."

There's a knock at the back door, and a woman enters. She says, "Anyone home?"

I hurry to the door, and Ned, the reporter, strides in.

She smiles and says, "Karina, good to see you."

Taken aback by her barging in, I bite my lip. I scold myself, because I forgot to lock the door when we came in from checking my car. Ned gives me a hug, and I squeeze her back. I respect her passion for getting bylines and covering the news. But if she is an indicator of outsiders being interested in the red notebook, I have a sinking feeling our town may soon be overrun with treasure hunters. Gobs of people want easy money. But if treasure is found and it is linked to Gigi, I will claim it as mine.

I step back and still my racing thoughts. This whole business has me going batty. I say, "Jeff said you might stop by."

She flashes a wide, white-toothed smile. "I'm working on a story about a missing journal. I heard you're at the hub of what's happening, and I'd like to interview you."

She turns to Mr. Frackus and thrusts out a hand. "I'm

Ned Bagley, a reporter for The Stranger." He introduces himself, and they shake hands.

She says, "I'm sorry to barge in on you and interrupt." To me, she says, "This story will interest readers. My editor loved the idea when I pitched it to him. The mystery of a relative's missing journal, set in a charming waterfront town in the San Juan Islands, will have wide appeal."

I arch an eyebrow. Millersville is located near the San Juan Islands in Washington State, but technically not in them. Our town is on a different island to the east. "That's stretching the truth a bit, isn't it?"

She shrugs. "It is just a working concept for now. We'll refine details and wordsmith closer to the deadline."

I cross my arms. I don't want her nosing into my business, and I need to send her back to Seattle. I really like her, and I admire her persistence, but not when she's about to pry into my personal life.

I say, "I can't see how a story like this would appeal to people in Seattle. There's a small item that has been misplaced. It is a sentimental memento. That won't interest readers."

She plops her purse onto a chair and frowns. "Jeff told me you were willing to talk."

I say, "It was a misunderstanding. I don't want to talk about my grandmother's journal. It's of interest to family members like me, but I'd rather not share information about it with the whole world. She only just died, after all."

"My condolences." She pats my elbow and pulls her phone from her pocket, reading a text. "Jeff said it was your grandmother's diary. So, it must mean a lot to you. Is that correct?"

I grind my teeth. She is hot on the trail of a new story and not stopping long to pay respects. The news comes first. Ned is pushy, and that is why she is one of the best in her field. When I recall Gigi's scribbled note about my having a sibling, I scrutinize Ned's face to see if we could be related. But then I stop myself from studying her features. I can't check every stranger's face for a resemblance. It would drive me crazy.

I tap my lips. But what about Violet? She has the same bump on her nose as I have. I shake off the thought. Violet grew up near Olympia, a few hours south. That is too far away. A sibling would have lived in the area when I was growing up. Wouldn't they?

I grimace. What if it was a child I went to grade school with? That would be creepy.

I gaze out the window into the alley. Did my mom have an affair and give birth to a baby who was adopted when I was too young to remember? She didn't seem like the type, but what do I know. With Gigi's secrets starting to spill out, I'm beginning to question everything I knew and was told.

Mr. Frackus says, "Karina, what do you think about what Ned just said?"

My eyes grow wide. "Sorry, I was lost in thought. What were you saying?"

She turns to me. "I'd like to sit and record our conversation? And by the way, the article could drum up interest, and perhaps bring in leads, to help you locate the diary. You'll end up getting more customers in the café with the publicity, I bet."

I let out an exasperated breath. "They'd snoop around, buy a cup of coffee, and spend hours asking questions. They'd bother my regular customers and get in the way. I don't think it's worth it."

She smiles. "I think you can manage that, if it happens. You're a strong, powerful, professional woman who runs her own business. You can handle a little extra foot traffic. And if it gets out of hand, you'll know how to shut it down. You're in charge, and I'm not asking you to do anything you're not comfortable with."

I eye her and consider what she said. She's buttering me up so she can get the story. Even though I'm aware of her tactics, her kind remarks put a dent in my resistance.

She holds up her hands. "And think about this. You haven't found the journal on your own, have you? Let the news bring out the culprit, so you can get Gigi's diary back. I suspect with my help, you'll get the journal back faster than if you work leads on your own. With Mr.

Frackus, that is. I mean, with the two of you working as a team."

I chew on the inside of my cheek. The two of us as a team? He's just helping me with my car and with the under the hairbrush clue. It would be weird to work with my science teacher. But come to think of it, Gigi would like it.

I let out a sigh. She makes a good point. I might as well participate and answer her questions. An article might draw out useful information and help the diary return to my house.

"Fine," I say, "I'll talk, but let's get this over with." I take a chair and turn it around. Plunking down, I face her with the back of the chair between us as a barrier.

She eyes our mugs of coffee. "Not to be a pain, but could I have some coffee? It was a long drive, and I'm dying for a caffeine fix."

Rising to pour her coffee, I know Gigi would scold me for my lack of manners. But I'm beginning to feel manipulated by Ned, and the interview hasn't even begun.

I set a mug down by her right hand. I want to get her out of here and start working on tracking down suspects. "Here you go."

She screws up her face. "I was hoping you might have a latte machine by now?"

Grinding my molars, I take a pitcher of cream from the refrigerator and plunk it down in front of her. "No latte machine. Not yet. Maybe not ever. There you go."

It's a classic city dweller versus small town resident conflict, right here in my kitchen, and I've got loads of other things on my list to do. Mr. Frackus, on the other hand, looks like he's settling in for a long while. He's smiling, as if this is the most interesting thing that's happened to him in many months.

She wrinkles her nose. "Remember, I don't drink that. Just soy milk."

I put the cream back in the frig.

She says to Mr. Frackus, "How are you involved in all this? Do you know who took the diary? And is it alright if I record our conversation?"

He nods.

"Great. I appreciate you talking with me. This could attract more tourists to your town."

I scowl. "We definitely do not need more tourists flocking here. We're overrun with them as it is."

17

While Ned sets up, I refill our coffees. Ned pulls her blond hair into a ponytail and rolls up her sleeves. She has a gleam in her eyes and looks ready for a challenge.

I sit down, drumming my fingers on the table. I want to get this over with. I plan to answer her questions as best I can. Then I'll focus on finding and interviewing suspects. My hands feel empty without holding the diary.

Seconds tick by. My tongue explores a gap between my front teeth. Did Gigi really take her money out of the bank and bury it? If so, it sounds risky. What if she forgot where she hid it?

I put my palms together. I must recover the journal and read what Gigi wrote. Perhaps it will provide clues and lead me to my unknown sibling.

My brow furrows. I can't believe I have a brother or a

sister, and no one told me before. I hate the fact that I was kept in the dark. Gigi should have trusted me with the earth-shaking news.

I scratch the back of my neck. Unless she was confused when she wrote that. If what she wrote is not true, then I don't have a mysterious sibling lurking somewhere.

I shift in my seat and massage my aching temples. All the breaking news and unveiled secrets is giving me a permanent headache. I could barely keep up with my new job of running the café. Now I must become an amateur sleuth and track down my grandmother's stolen notebook.

Mr. Frackus removes his blue sport coat and hangs it on the back of the chair.

Ned sets her phone to record and rests it on the table. Her pink phone cover sparkles.

I cross my arms. Her latte comment and glittering phone cover grate at me. Sometimes, even when you admire someone and like them as a friend, they get on your nerves, and that is exactly what Ned is doing now. What makes her a consummate professional and good at her job is rubbing me the wrong way.

Ned says, "Thank you for speaking with me. Let's get started. Please state your names and occupations."

"Karina Walker, artist and current owner of Gigi's Cafe."

"Bernard Frackus, retired teacher."

She says, "Karina, I understand your grandmother's

journal is missing from the café. What did the journal look like?"

"It has a red leather cover, and it's about this big." I hold up my hands, indicating the dimensions.

For the next twenty minutes, Mr. Frackus and I tell our stories. We take a quick break for Ned to use the bathroom. When she comes back, I mention how the journal is of sentimental importance and it matters a lot to me because it was my grandmother's.

"But it is not just a keepsake," Ned says, "is it? From what I heard, it holds clues to what could be a cache of hidden money."

I throw my hands up in the air. "Please don't print that, whatever you do. I don't want swarms of treasure seekers pounding on the doors at all times of day and night. I can just imagine people walking the perimeter of the house using metal detectors or digging holes in the yard."

Mr. Frackus rubs his chin. "She's right. It would attract the nut cases and people who are drawn to mysteries. Please, don't print that. It is pure speculation."

I nod. "Thank you, Mr. Frackus."

He says, "I think it's time you started calling me Bernard."

I tilt my head. "It feels wrong, but maybe in time, I'll do that. Let me think about it." To Ned, I say, "You see, he was my high school science teacher."

Ned's eyes light up. "Wait a minute. You two are a team, working together to solve the mystery of the missing diary? And he was your teacher? What's the connection between you two?"

I shrug. I guess we are a team, now that I think about it. I need help, and he offered it. Maybe we can solve this together.

I say, "He and my grandmother were friends."

He wipes a tear from his eye and clears his throat. "Very good friends."

Ned leans in. "I like that senior sweetheart aspect to the story. Readers will eat this up."

My fingers turn cold. "We're private people," I say. "We don't want details about our personal lives plastered all over the paper and on socials."

She sighs and sips coffee. "Fine, fine. I'll leave that out for now. But I may be back later as a follow up or for a separate story. Now, back to business. Where exactly was the diary before it was taken?"

I say, "It was hidden in a dining room drawer, but then it disappeared. And a lot of people were here on Friday afternoon. That's the end of the story. I've got a lot to do, and we need to wrap this up."

Ned stands. "Is it all right if I go in the dining room? It'll help me fill in details if I can see where it was taken."

"I need to clarify though, that I'm not absolutely sure it was stolen," I say. "It might've been misplaced, or it could have been thrown out. In fact, I need to go through the dumpster out back and check. This all could be a blown-up mistake, and it could be right in the alley. I just haven't gotten around to it."

Ned says, "Let's go in the dining room. It won't take long."

"I'll give you five more minutes, max," I say. "Then I need to get to work. The scones are calling. They don't make themselves, you know."

Mr. Frackus says to me, "I can help you make scones."

I nod. His company would be welcome. He seems like a kind man who wants to make my life better, like a fairy godfather. We could refine the list of suspects and eliminate some. Right now, I have too many people in mind to make finding the journal manageable.

"Thanks," I tell him. "I could use your help."

Ned looks at the two of us. "I could hang out and listen to what you talk about. It would just be background for the story. I wouldn't have to record it."

I bite my lip. I have got to nip her sleuthing skills in the bud. If I don't, everything I say will end up in print. I just want to live a quiet creative life and follow through with my promise to my grandmother. I don't want mayhem and madness around the old house where I live, or for treasure seekers and gold diggers to hound me.

I lead her into the dining room. "I'll pass on that. I wouldn't do well being observed and listened to while I work. Besides, I only need Bernard's help. But feel free to come in the café while you're in town for quiche and scones."

"Understood," she says, scanning the room. "So, this is where it all went down? Which drawer was it?"

I walk over and open a drawer. My mouth falls open. It is empty.

I say in a quiet voice, "This drawer was jam-packed with papers earlier today when we went upstairs to search my grandmother's bedroom."

Bernard nods.

I doubt he would have taken them. I eye her messenger bag. She wants the story. She is motivated. She stepped away to use the restroom and was alone in the rest of the house for a few minutes.

I say, "I'd like to check your bag and see what's in it. Some of my things are missing."

She hugs it to her chest. "I wouldn't take anything."

I tap my foot. I let the diary slip out of my hands once. I won't let more of Gigi's precious papers go and repeat my mistake again.

She shrugs and opens the bag. "Fine, take a look. But I didn't do it. I just got here."

Her notebook is in there and her cell. She doesn't have my grandmother's papers.

"I'm sorry, but I had to ask." I stifle a yawn. "I don't understand how the drawer was cleaned out while we were in the house."

"It certainly is mysterious," Bernard says. "And very concerning."

Ned says, "You'd better lock your doors. I guess small towns aren't as safe as I thought."

"It is," I say, walking her to the back door. "I just hit a weird spot after Gigi passed. I'm rowing up a river against the current. It's not normally like this."

She laughs. "That's what you said when the peaceful protests turned into riots."

I shrug. "I swear, our town is safe. I'm just attracting the wrong element for some weird reasons I can't figure out yet. Good luck with your story."

"If the paper runs this story above the fold," she says, "I'll be dancing on my desk."

After she leaves, Bernard and I wipe down the kitchen counters, wash pots and pans, and empty the dishwasher. It's odd, having him here and also calming to be in his presence. Because Gigi gave him the letter for me, I trust him.

Putting away silverware, forks clank as they nest against each other.

I say, "I wonder who came in and emptied the drawer in the dining room? Do you have any ideas?" A thought occurs to me, and I stare at him. "You didn't do it, did you?"

He wipes his hands on a dish towel. "Heck, no, I would never do that. But someone is messing with you and your things. I think you should call the police."

"I'm not sure they'd be interested. It's just a journal."

"One that means a lot to you. One that someone may have taken."

I pick up my phone and dial 911. "I'm calling to report a theft."

The dispatcher takes down details and says an officer will stop by.

While we wait for the police to arrive, we prepare scone dough and put it in the refrigerator to chill. I'll bake them before the sun rises. Owning an early morning business is foreign for me. In Seattle, when I wasn't temping in an office, I slept in and arrived at the art studio around eleven.

Mr. Frackus wipes flour from his nose. "I always wanted to help your grandmother in the kitchen, but she wouldn't let me. She made me sit and watch."

When the doorbell rings, I hurry to the front door.

Two Millersville police officers in blue uniforms stand on the front porch.

"Please come in."

A female officer with short brown hair says, "You reported that something was stolen?"

"Yes, my grandmother's diary and some papers."

Her partner puts his hands on his hips. "Tell us what happened."

I guide them to the dining room and point to the drawers.

"My grandmother left a diary in that drawer. I saw it Friday afternoon when the place was packed. A customer pulled it out and showed it to me. She was supposed to leave it on the table, but when I checked later on, it was gone. The rest of the contents of the drawer were removed after that. I saw papers in there earlier today."

The two officers exchange a quick glance.

"Let me get this straight," the woman says. "A diary was in the drawer on Friday afternoon. And someone took it, you think. They came back and stole what was left in the drawer?"

I nod. "That's right."

"How many people have keys to this house?" the man asks.

"Just me."

I glance at Mr. Frackus, wondering who else has an entry key. My grandmother was known for trusting others and giving out house keys like they were Christmas cookies. She said it was in case a friend went shopping for her, so they could put the milk away. Or if a friend bought flour in bulk, they could leave it in the kitchen. Or if a neighbor was hungry for a scone while Gigi was out running errands on a day she was closed.

"My cousin Lydia has a key. And my Aunt Jean has one."

"I have one," Mr. Frackus says. "Gigi gave it to me, so I could fix the coffee maker when it went on the blink."

The female officer says, "It sounds like a lot of people have access to the building. They could've come in and taken the journal when you weren't here."

I grimace. Or when I was here. When I was asleep or soaking in the bathtub.

"Have you left the premises since Friday afternoon?"

"Yes, I went to see Kenny Robinson at his sporting goods store. I stopped by Ellie Robinson's to talk with her because they were here when it disappeared. I went to see Boots Brinker and her dad. Boots opened that drawer and found the journal. I met Wanda Robinson at Starbuck's. Oh, and I went to see Mr. Frackus."

"And a reporter from Seattle was here," Mr. Frackus says.

I say, "I checked, but she didn't have the papers in her bag."

"So, any number of people could have come in while you were gone."

I shift my weight from side to side. I'm boxed in by the bare facts, and it is making me uncomfortable. The way it sounds, I've given the whole town access to my home and business. My face heats. I stare at the glass knobs on the built-in drawer.

"Is the item valuable?" she says.

"It is to me. The journal was my grandmother's, and she raised me. By reading it, I hope I'll learn more about her and what she was like before I came along."

The officer nods and looks at her partner.

He says, "It sounds like a sentimental item and not worth a lot of money. Unfortunately, we don't have much to go on."

Secrets at the Café 141

She looks me in the eye. "We'll make a report and see what we can do. But it's unlikely we'll recover it. A journal compared to people reporting stolen cars and catalytic converters won't get much attention at the station."

He nods. "We'll let you know if we uncover new information. In the meantime, change the locks on your doors, so no one can get in. Burglaries are on the rise this year, especially in this neighborhood."

Walking them to the door, I say, "Thank you for coming by. I hope you'll find the journal. Maybe someone will turn it into the police station."

"It's always a possibility," she says.

I close the door and lean against it. "At least I filed a report, in case someone turns it in. But I doubt the police will uncover it. I need to identify the culprit."

Mr. Frackus adjusts his glasses. "I've got the time. Let's do this."

Smiling, I say, "We'll bring the diary back to the café, where it belongs. But before we get started, I want to change the locks on the doors."

18

M r. Frackus and I drive in his car to Ace Hardware, where I buy door locks.

While we install a new Schlage lock on the front door, I say, "Because we're working together to find the diary, I'm going to try calling you by your first name. We'll see if it sticks."

He sets down a screwdriver. "That'd be fine. My name is Bernard, but your grandmother had a special nickname for me."

I cover my ears. I need some semblance of separation between the Gigi I knew and the one he dated.

"I don't want to hear it."

I turn the lock and test it, clicking it open and closed. I smile. I'll be safe inside from now on. "This one works. Let's move on to the next door. And by the way, I appreciate you helping me."

"I didn't have anything pressing," he says. "Gigi would've wanted me to make sure you're safe."

We replace the lock on the back door, and I dust off my hands. "I've got an idea. Let's check online to see if anyone's selling the diary. I'll use my laptop, and we'll go on eBay, Craigslist, and Etsy."

Heading into the kitchen, I spot a brown paper bag on the floor in the corner, leaning against the wall. The sack is stuffed full of papers.

I say, "Who left this?"

I pick up the bag and set it on the table, spreading out the contents. A pink envelope catches my eye. On Friday after I closed the cafe, I checked to see if Boots had tucked the journal in the drawer. That's when I saw the pink envelope. It was there this morning too when I looked.

Bernard leans over the table, giving off the scent of Old Spice aftershave.

I tap the pink envelope with an index finger. Potters avoid long fingernails, because they get in the way when throwing pots and make stray marks in clay. Mine are trimmed short, ready to work in mud. I wish I was throwing bowls on my wheel now, instead of uncovering secrets and searching for a notebook I never should have let leave the house.

I say, "These papers were kept where the journal was stored. I wonder who did this? Did we interrupt someone in the act or did they bring them back?"

He says, "It could've been anyone."

My pulse quickens. Someone came in my house while I was out. I wonder if I'm safe, even with new door locks. I pick up the pink envelope.

He says, "I hope that isn't a letter from one of your grandmother's early suitors. It would hurt too much." He scratches his salt and pepper whiskered chin.

I cock my head. "Who were her early suitors?"

"She told me about a Canadian Royal Mounted Policeman, a Mountie."

"Ooh, interesting. Who were the others?"

"That's a discussion for another day. It would be, as younger people say, TMI. But I add an A. TMIA."

I laugh. "What's the 'A' stand for?"

"I made it up," he smiles. "Stands for too much information all at once."

"Sounds doubly bad."

I open the pink envelope. We're treating it like it has kryptonite inside, but it can't rock my world. Gigi's death already did that, leaving me orphaned all over again.

Inside, I find a phone number scrawled on a wrinkled piece of paper.

I say, "The phone number has our area code. She scribbled someone's name. Bill Rafferty. Do you know who he is?"

Bernard looks down. His face turns pale.

I turn the name over in my mind but don't recall Gigi mentioning this man. Fumbling with my phone, I look him up on Google. Nothing matches a person Gigi would know. Men with that name are on the East Coast, posing with boats in photos.

Scrolling down, my eyes widen. There's a Bill Rafferty who lives in Millersville, and he's a pawn broker. "Why would Gigi have his phone number?"

Bernard clears his throat. "Your father, as a police officer, arrested him for something shady. He ended up testifying against him in court."

I break out in a sweat. "Are you saying the car crash was intentional? That Bill Rafferty could have killed my parents?"

He nods.

My stomach sours, and I rest a hand on it. "Why didn't I know about this?"

He put his hands on the table, fingers splayed out. "Gigi wanted to protect you, so she never told you what she suspected about the car accident. She told me I could share it with you if you ever asked. But the important thing to remember is, we aren't sure Bill Rafferty was involved. Some people in town don't like him because they owe him money. Someone else may have caused the car crash, but a few folks placed the blame on him because he's an easy target."

I gnaw on a fingernail. "Why didn't my parents go into the witness protection program? Could they have moved, gone into hiding, and changed their names?"

"It wasn't an option. Your father was a police officer. That was his job."

With a sigh, I get up to fill two glasses with water, giving Bernard one. Drinking mine down, I lean against the counter. He tips the glass back and empties his.

I nod, mulling all of this over. During college I read an article saying successful women tend to have close relationships with their maternal grandmothers. Gigi was my bedrock, and that is why I'm doing my best to fulfill her penultimate and final requests. Return home to run the café, and read the diary. My eyes rest on my grandmother's handwriting with the man's name and phone number.

"But why did she have Bill Rafferty's number? How did she know him?"

Bernard waves a hand. "I would just forget about it."

"You're probably right." But before I toss it in the wastebasket under the kitchen sink, I memorize the phone number. I may want to contact him and glean information from him in the future. "Coffee?"

"Yes, please."

Grinding the beans, I inhale a rich, nutty aroma. I pour water into the pot and add a filter, dumping in coffee grounds and closing the lid. The smell of coffee fills the kitchen. I usually enjoy waiting for the first cup from a fresh-brewed pot. It is a time of possibility and anticipating delicious tastes ahead. Now I fidget with my fingers and pace the kitchen.

I say, "Please, tell me anything else you know about my parents and Rafferty."

He rubs his forehead. "I heard he wasn't sentenced for that crime. They couldn't prove he was involved."

The coffee maker beeps.

He gets up, pats me on the shoulder, and pours two cups.

A spear of guilt stabs me. I have been complaining about being overworked in a place where I was loved. It is my time to return the favor and stop being self-centered.

Bernard coughs. "Bill knew your dad. It was part of your father's work."

I purse my lips. "So, we don't know if Bill Rafferty had a hand in my parents' deaths. Or why Gigi was in touch with him. If I ever get the chance to meet him, I'll ask him why my grandmother had his number."

"Please, let go of it. Let's check eBay and Craigslist. Weren't we going to do that?"

I open the laptop and we look online for a while, finding nothing. But then I blow out a breath. What I've learned so far has been overwhelming. and I need time alone.

I say, "It's getting late, and I'm worn out. How about we do this another time?"

"I understand."

At the door, I say, "Thank you for telling me what you know."

"I'll be straight with you," he says. "Good night."

He closes the door behind him, and I lock the door.

19

After Bernard leaves, I eat a few bites of peanut butter. I pull out my green potter's apron and tie it around my waist. Tears stream down my cheeks, wishing for my missing family members to be with me. Picking up a cardboard box with my art supplies, I lug it to the top of the basement stairs.

I balance the box on my hip and flip on the light switch. I haven't been down to the basement since I moved home. Now it's time to face my fear of dark places and huge, hairy spiders, and my disgust with dank smells. Opening the door, a dusty bulb in the stairwell gives off a high-pitched whine.

Sucking in my stomach, I pick up the box and start down the stairs, taking one step at a time to avoid falling. The basement creeps me out. It's been like that since I was a child. Fetid air smells like something died down here. I breathe through my mouth.

Three large rooms are on the unfinished lower level. In the middle of the biggest room is an old well with a round cement cover. A dingy bathroom at the far end has a toilet, a shower stall, and a sink.

I recall when I was a child and the other two bathrooms in the house were in use. Gigi told me to use the one in the basement. Down I went, step by step, to meet my fate. Cool air cloaked my skin. I shivered as I went deeper into the basement.

I tiptoed over to the basement bathroom and opened the door. The hinges squealed. My arm brushed against the plastic shower curtain, and I jumped away and screamed.

Gigi came rushing downstairs to rescue me.

I hugged her tight. "Don't make me use that bathroom ever again."

"We'll wait until you're older and braver," she said, guiding me upstairs.

Now that I'm older, I must be brave. The basement is the best place in the house for my art studio. If clay splats or paint flies, it won't matter down here. No guests will see it. What was spooky will become my private creative sanctuary.

I reach the bottom step. A mouse skitters across the floor, I drop the box, spewing the contents all over the cold cement floor.

With a shaky voice, I say, "I'm taking this over. The space is mine. Get out now if you know what's good for you."

Scanning the largest room, I notice most of the light bulbs are burned out. I also need to sweep and wet mop the floor. I nod, imagining making clay sculptures, throwing pots on the wheel, and painting on canvases. When I save enough, I'll buy an electric kiln and hire an electrician to upgrade the junction box. I'd risk an electrical fire if I plugged in a kiln now and fired it with our current system. Potters like fire but not that kind of a blaze.

Turning on music to calm my nerves, I hurry upstairs to the pantry and grab new lightbulbs. Back in the basement, I use a stepstool and change the bulbs. Light floods the space, pushing away the scary shadows.

Dust swirls when I sweep the floor, and I cough. I dip a sponge in a bucket of warm water with lemon-scented Pine-Sol and scrub window ledges. The water is dirty gray when I pour it into the toilet and flush. I wet mop the floor, working up a sweat.

I drag my potter's wheel over to a window, making a scraping sound, and step back and smile.

"Now for the shelves," I say.

I stack heavy cinder blocks, humming as I work. I insert two-by-fours to create shelves and slap pieces of plywood onto the makeshift shelves.

"Things are looking up," I say. "Even though I'm in a spooky basement. Ma, ha, ha. But I can handle it."

I set up my easel and rest an unfinished abstract painting on it. The background is a wash of blues and greens. I set up a folding table and wipe the surface with Windex. Then I open my brush holder and place my favorite paint brushes side by side, like old friends, alongside pots of acrylic paint.

Putting my hands on my hips, I look around. This room will be my respite. Instead of serving endless scones, coffee, and quiches, a work of art will remain at the end of a day.

I open my arms. "This is the private studio I have always wanted. A sacred space to make art. And it is all my own."

My phone dings with a text upstairs, and I charge up the steps. I left it upstairs to avoid distractions, like Wanda and I talked about, while setting up my studio.

Wanda texted. "How's it going? Are you meditating? Did you set up your art studio yet?"

I grin and text back. "Art studio looks good. But I need to meditate more. Did you try writing in bursts?"

"Yep, it's helping. More later."

"Thanks for checking in."

I bring the spray bottle of Windex upstairs and turn the lights out in the basement. My grandmother was a fan of using Windex, and the smell reminds me of her. A knot in my chest holds my sadness. If only I had told her more often how much I loved her, and how I appreciated all she did for me. She sacrificed her dating life.

Someone knocks at the back door, and I stride over to see who it is.

Lydia and Shane are looking in, grinning and waving.

I'd forgotten about my promise for them to hang out here a second evening.

Opening the door wide, I say, "Come on in. We can have popcorn again if you like."

Lydia says, "And watch another movie."

"How about Spider-Man?" Shane says. "No Way Home."

I say, "Perfect."

We sit on the sofa, sharing a big bowl of salted popcorn and crunching in unison. I don't breathe a word of what I learned from Mr. Frackus, I mean Bernard, about my grandmother's relationship. I'll tell Lydia in time, but it is way too soon. I need to process what I heard. And I might want to track down Bill Rafferty and hear what he has to say for himself.

Later, after they leave, I climb into bed and pull the covers up. My life is turning around. I have an art studio. I have a home and a business. I can do this. I just need to find the journal.

Tomorrow, I must wade through the trash bin out back, in case the diary was thrown out. I hope I'll be able to read Gigi's handwriting if food scraps are splatted all over the pages.

I smile. I can run the café. My grandmother taught me how. I will trust my instincts and let my hands follow the motions she showed me. Make scone dough. Form into wedges. Chill for better results. Roll out dough for quiche crusts. Fry the bacon and break into chunks. Prepare the quiche filling.

Snuggling under the covers, I sigh. I was loved by my parents and grandmother. Bill Rafferty is a question mark in my investigation. I want to meet him and talk with him.

20

The following morning, on Monday, I detach the trickle charger and start my car, letting it run in the alley to be sure the battery is charged. I go inside and check emails. A few minutes later, with a crash and a bang, the garbage truck charges down the alley, aiming for the dumpster out back.

I moan and run out in my slippers, waving, and gesturing for the driver to stop the truck. The journal might be in the dumpster. I forgot to sort through the stinky mess. I should have tackled that task earlier this morning before taking my first sip of coffee. But I put it off.

The driver brakes and comes to a stop. Randy, as usual, is covering the route. He comes in for coffee and a scone on his breaks.

I put my palms together. "Could you please come back

in fifteen minutes? Something precious might've been thrown away." I point to the dumpster. "I need to sort through the trash before you take it."

"Sorry, I'm on a tight schedule."

"Please, it won't take long. I'll work fast."

He's quiet for a moment, and then he smiles. "What the heck. I might have hell to pay, but I'll come back. But get in there and dig. Work fast. I'm almost finished with this part of my route. You have ten minutes max."

A grin spreads across my face. "Thank you so much, and I owe you a month's worth of free scones, quiche, and coffee."

"It's a deal."

He gives me a nod before backing up and driving away in a cloud of dust.

Minutes tick by as I haul the bags out and paw through them. My fingers are covered with damp coffee grounds, bits of uneaten quiche, and baked goods. No signs of a red diary so far.

In the last bag, a crumpled piece of paper attracts my attention. I unfold it. It's a grocery list with Gigi's handwriting at the bottom.

In her flowery cursive writing, it says, "Look under the microwave for a token of my love."

I shake my head. How did this end up in the trash? I stuff the note in my back pocket.

Going in the kitchen, I wash quiche-scone-jam sticky residue off my hands. I lift the microwave, set it aside, and pick up an envelope. Opening it, I find a card decorated with a drawing of a tabby cat.

I blink back tears and open the card.

"Dear Kit Kat, I hope this finds you in better spirits than when I last saw you, after you broke up with Jeff. I want you to have the most prosperous life possible, so look on the back for instructions to your own personal gold mine."

Tilting my head, I wonder if my grandmother had fun when she left notes scattered around the house for me to find, or if she was getting daffy. Maybe it was a bit of both. She had a gleam in her eyes when we did treasure hunts on Sundays, and the café was closed. It's almost as if she is still alive. Her spirit certainly is, given how many notes she sprinkled around the place.

Outside, the garbage truck pulls up and picks up the dumpster. With a bang and a clang, the lid closes, and Randy takes off down the alley. At least I checked all the bags. No red journal was hidden inside.

I turn the card over and clap a hand to my chest. I'm holding a money order made out to me for five hundred dollars. How could she afford to give me this much money?

I tuck the money order in my front pocket and glance around. I'm ill prepared to open the café tomorrow morning. Tables need to be set. I must roll out scone dough to refrigerate and bake them in the morning. A mouth-watering smell will waft through the cafe tomorrow, making Eleanor Peterson moan when she walks in promptly at seven o'clock.

I pull Gigi's apron over my head and get to work. She was a wonder, managing the cafe with a willing ear to listen to anyone's troubles. She deserved a heroine's medal.

I take scone dough from the frig and slam the door shut with my foot. "Gigi, you are my hero. I should've told you that."

An hour later, I place plates of scone dough wedges in the refrigerator.

Bernard raps at the back door.

Going over, I open the door. "Good to see you. Come on in."

"I was running errands and thought I'd check in with you. Any progress?"

"Not yet. But my car starts, thanks to your help. You can take your trickle charger back."

Dirty dishes cover the kitchen counter, but I ignore them. "Let's see if someone is selling a worn red leather journal. If it's from the 1980s, it might be Gigi's."

"You search online," he says. "I'll do the dishes."

Sitting at the kitchen table, I tap on my laptop.

He tackles the pots and pans. As he scrubs, metal hits metal, sounding like a gong.

I check Etsy, eBay, and Craigslist. But I don't find a red journal. I'm about to give up when a last search result catches my eye.

"Diary for sale," I say, turning to him. "Look at this."

It seems strange to call him by his first name because he was my high school teacher. It's tough to dislodge my memory from our formal relationship. It's hard to believe he was my grandmother's lover, but he knows too much about her and my family to be faking it.

He comes over and reads the laptop screen. Drying his hands on a dish cloth, he says, "Looks promising. Let's see if it's the real thing or a waste of time."

Clicking on the link, I point to the screen and read aloud.

"Pre-owned Vintage Leather Journal for sale. Learn about the toll the 2009 Great Recession took on a family first-hand."

"Wrong time period," I say. "Too recent. But strikingly similar."

He nods. "And it's got a green cover. Are you sure it was red? And was the page Boots and you read from the 1980s, not something more recent?"

"I'm sure it had a red leather cover. The page I read was from a Monday in 1987, when the stock market crashed."

He goes back to the sink. "Then we're still on the hunt. After this bowl, I'd best be off."

I study his back. He might want the diary as a token to remember my grandmother.

"Why do you want to find the journal?" I say. "Surely you have better things to do?"

He clears his throat and glances out the kitchen window.

I chastise myself for making a mistake. I've been rude to the one person in town who has offered to help me. Well, except for Lydia, that is.

I say, "Sorry, I didn't mean to offend you. I really appreciate everything you're doing for me."

"I loved your grandmother, and I strongly believe her private thoughts shouldn't be hung out in public. After all, she isn't here to stand up for herself."

I nod. Her diary being pawed over by a stranger would be a violation of her privacy.

"I agree, and I can see why my grandmother liked you."

He gives me a weak smile.

My stomach growls.

When he leaves, taking the trickle charger with him, I cook scrambled eggs and toast. Then I preheat the oven, fry bacon, and grate cheddar cheese.

Mixing eggs with half-and-half, I use Gigi's recipe for the quiche filling. She used three eggs to one and a half cups half-and-half. Adding shredded cheese and bacon chunks to the eggs, I sprinkle in dried parsley, basil, and dill, along salt and fresh ground pepper. One day I might add wilted spinach or mushrooms, but for now, I'm sticking to Gigi's recipes.

I fill the pre-baked quiche crusts with the mixture and slide them into the oven. When the timer dings, I rest the baked quiches on the stove top to cool. Four will be enough for tomorrow. Customers order three and a half quiches' worth on a typical day.

Feeling good about my preparations for when the café opens tomorrow, I go down to my art studio. I work on an abstract painting until a series of yawns overtakes me. The day has flown by, and it's time to go to bed.

I tromp up to the first floor and check the door locks. Climbing into bed, I pull the white comforter over me and sink back onto my pillow.

The wind picks up outside, whistling through cracks in the window. Boards holding up the place groan with complaints. Trees moan, swishing in the wind.

I could use the gift from Gigi to remove moss from the steep roof. I could buy a second dishwasher. I could save up to purchase a pre-owned electric kiln to fire pottery.

Tears of gratitude trickle down my cheeks. I am not alone. Bernard Frackus is helping me search for the diary. Lydia and Shane went to the pool party to help me find it. Randy gave me time to search through the garbage.

Looking up at the ceiling, I smile. My grandmother had a secret lover.

"Good for you, Gigi," I say. "You deserved all the love in the world."

21

My alarm goes off at four the next morning, and I shut it off. I stay in bed with my eyes closed, listening to the sounds of an old house. Wind whooshes past. Windows rattle in their frames. A tree branch rubs against the siding. The building groans.

A coffee cup clatters in the kitchen.

My eyes open wide. Someone is in my home. I leap out of bed, heart thudding.

Floorboards creak down on the first floor.

Pulling on my robe, I fly down the stairs and into the kitchen. The lights are on, and I'm greeted by the smell of coffee.

My aunt Jean brushes the bangs out of her eyes and gives me a broad smile. "You're up. I've been getting things ready for you before you open. Given the way Lydia has been flitting about, I thought you could use the help."

I clap a hand to my chest. "You gave me a fright. I'm glad it was you and not a burglar."

"Just family, trying to help."

I cinch the robe tight around my waist and glance around the kitchen. "But how did you get in? I changed the locks and haven't had time to give you a new key."

She points to a window. "I crawled in through that big sash window. The latch doesn't work. That's how I got in as a teenager. I pried it open this morning when my key didn't work in the door."

I rest a shaky hand on the counter to steady myself. This is not my normal morning routine, where I move like a snail and slowly wake up. Compared to this bus station of a house, where people are tromping in and out day and night, my life in Seattle was a muffled cocoon of stillness. Well, except for when I sold at art fairs. Then pandemonium reigned, and anything could happen.

One time, a shopping cart with a little girl in the front was rolling down a slope toward me at an outdoor show. I looked around for an adult who must be with the child but didn't see anyone. When the cart was a few inches from knocking over my wire mesh booth with all my pottery, I snaked out a hand, stopping it just in time, saving my wares and the little girl from harm. But I'm no heroine. I'm just an ordinary person trying to make her way in the world.

I come back to the present and focus my gaze on my aunt. "I appreciate you coming over. Thanks."

She hands me a cup of coffee. "Take this upstairs with you and get changed. While the scones bake, you can tell me all that you know about my mother's journal. I'd like to learn more about it. I haven't read it."

I sink down into a chair. "I need a few moments first before I go up. I had a scare, hearing someone in the house. I didn't know it was you."

She slides into a seat opposite me at the kitchen table. We sip coffee in silence for a few minutes. Clutching the warm cup, I inhale coffee-scented steam and review what just happened. It was only my aunt. It's okay. I'm safe. I don't need to freak out about every little noise in the house. I need to fix the window latch.

Letting out a sigh, I decide to start my morning over with a fresh mind set. Being jittery and on edge is not good for my health and would carry over to interactions with guests, irritating them and giving them a negative experience. I don't want to jinx the gift my guardian gave me. Not many people are willed a going business entity and a family home. I'm not perfect as a café owner or a professional restauranteur, but the opportunities she left me are pretty close to a sweet situation, if I can find it in my heart to accept my new path in life. Glancing around the kitchen, I reflect that I may be inching toward acceptance. Having help from my aunt, and Bernard, and others is pushing me toward the imaginary finish line of starting over.

"Sorry I rattled you," she says. "The place must be awfully quiet without my mother around. She had a way of making everyone comfortable." She sighs.

"It does feel spooky at times." I take a sip and breathe in the aroma of the dark roast. "Especially at night. And in the early mornings, when no one else is awake in town. I really do appreciate you coming over."

My aunt sets down her cup and fixes her gaze on me. "And I'm happy to help you. I have an idea. You know what you could do? You should sell the house and move in with Lydia and me. You'd have your own room in the basement."

I shiver and rub my arms. "Thanks, that's kind of you to offer, but basements aren't places I like to be." Then I think of my artist studio in the basement below us and smile. "Besides, I told Gigi I'd run the cafe, and I've got to keep my word. She'd roll over in her grave if I sold the place."

She makes a circle with her index finger on the table. "In my opinion, you don't have to keep a death bed promise. You said what she wanted to hear, and it made her happy at the end. She won't know if you don't follow through. And I think taking on this place is a lot for you to handle. I can't imagine how stressful it's been for you to move home and manage this place on your own."

I purse my lips. "But I'd know if I didn't keep my

promise to her. I wouldn't feel right about it. It would hang over my head, and I'd feel like I did something wrong. It would mean I lied to her on her last day, and I couldn't live with that."

My aunt shrugs. "But she's gone. You can do whatever you want and lead your life the way you like. Your promise made her happy before she passed. That's all that matters."

I gulp. "I can't ignore the promise I made. The café meant everything to her. I have to keep my word. She changed her life for me and took me in when my parents died. The least I can do is pay her back, even though she won't see it with her own eyes."

She says, "Okay, but if you ever change your mind, I will support your decision to sell and move back to the city."

I nod. Sticking with what I said to Gigi is the right choice for me. I couldn't live with myself otherwise. Another person might change the rules after a person dies and disregard a deathbed promise, but I can't. I've got to follow my own rule book.

Gigi taught me to keep my word, be on time, and tell the truth. Her guidance sounded simple and straight forward, at least that's what I thought as a child, but I've learned it isn't always easy to carry out in real life. I'll follow my internal compass on this issue, even though my aunt firmly disagrees. Family and friends can offer opinions, but I'm the one who must live with my final decisions. I wouldn't get any sleep at night if I betrayed my beloved, departed guardian.

Aunt Jean says, "I wish Lydia and I could have been with you on the day my mom died. That was a lot for you to shoulder on your own."

I let out a sigh. "I knew you couldn't leave your former mother-in-law. You promised to watch over her. She couldn't be alone in her house. It just worked out that way, is all. And no matter who was there, it would've been tough to take."

She nods. "That's right. Gigi also told me she wanted time alone with you at the end. We'd been over there so much, and we'd said our goodbyes. It was a rough time."

I swallow tears and set my cup on the counter. "It was. I'll take a shower and be right down."

I head upstairs and step into the shower. Water sprays my face, and I scrub with soap, preparing for a new day of being in service to hungry customers. While I towel dry, a thought crosses my mind. My aunt may have taken the journal to keep her mother's memory close. Or she might want it to solve the mystery in the diary about a hidden hoard of money. I can understand why she would want it.

I make a face and tell myself to get real. No one in my family is a thief. Aunt Jean and Lydia know I'm looking for it. They wouldn't keep it a secret and hide it from me.

Going down to the kitchen in jeans and a sweatshirt, I find my aunt arranging scone dough on baking sheets.

She slides two pans into the hot oven. She helped my grandmother when she was young, so she's a pro.

I pour a cup of coffee.

She beams at me. "I hope you'll have enough food today. I have a feeling everyone will be stopping by to ask about the missing journal. This will be good for business."

The smell of baking scones fills the room. This has to be my favorite smell in the whole world.

I say, "You're right. Tons more people might come in. If you have time, let's mix up another batch of scone dough and chill it, in case I run out. But I hope I don't have to spend my day answering questions from nosy people who are just popping in to gossip."

"Well, that's the price of running a small business, I'd say. And you should be grateful for the extra clientele, if it materializes. Rake it in while you can. And do whatever it takes." My aunt scrubs a mixing bowl and stops to stare at me. "You didn't take the journal and stick it somewhere as a publicity stunt, did you? To drum up more business?"

I snort. "No way. I can barely keep up with the way things are. I don't need more customers knocking at my door."

She studies me for a moment. "I believe you, but you'd better be prepared for people asking you that question. If I thought of it, you can be sure others will too."

I open the frig and pull out what we need to make scones. Kicking the door shut, I say, "Great, just what I need, being blamed for rumors flying around town that I had nothing to do with. I should never have let it out of my sight."

"Hey, don't blame yourself. Gigi wouldn't. You're doing your best to get it back."

I glance at the ceiling. "I'm not so sure about that. I think this time, if she was alive, she'd scold me for being careless and turning my back on a precious item. She always said I was too distracted. She called me her artful butterfly, flitting around. I've got to get it back."

Aunt Jean says, "You'll find it, I'm sure of it. Now let's make the scones."

We mix the dough and put it in the refrigerator.

I say, "It's nice to know I don't have to do this alone. Thanks for your help,'"

"Call or text me if you need me. I'll come wait tables or wash dishes if I'm not meeting with a customer."

She wraps me in a warm hug, and I lean into her, appreciating the support.

She steps back. "Wait, before I go, tell me more about the diary. Rumors are flying around that my mom had a map showing buried treasure, and it involves a scavenger hunt. Is that in any way connected to the facts?"

I laugh. "That's absurd. People are getting carried away."

I lean against the counter and quickly review what happened on Friday. I bring her up to date with details about Bernard Frackus, Ned the reporter, and the empty drawer in the dining room.

She clears the table and sets our mugs down in the sink with a thud. "My mom and Mr. Frackus were going out? I had no idea. They sure were sneaky."

Holding up my hands, I say, "It was a surprise to me too."

She rubs her temples. "No wonder he wanted to visit her when she was in hospice. I told him only family were allowed at her bedside. I should have let him in."

I bite my lip. The poor man, shut out from contact with a loved one at the last minute. That must have been awful for him.

"But we didn't know. I wish Gigi would've told me." A thought crosses my mind. "What if he's making this up to get his hands on her journal, and he's going to sell it? Or he wants to read it because he had a one-sided crush on her? We only have his word about their relationship."

She drums her fingers on the counter. "I did see him hanging out over here over the years. They'd sit in the back yard on a blanket having a picnic, instead of going to a park. But I didn't put it together that they were in love. I should have."

I say, "It sounds like they were secretive. I wanted to ask you something. Do you know why Gigi had Bill Rafferty's phone number? Is there a reason she'd want to call him?"

She stows her coffee cup in the dishwasher. "I have no idea. I've got to run home and make Lydia's breakfast now. Not that she eats it, but I feel better offering her a plate of scrambled eggs before she runs out the door for school. Teenagers, you know?"

I walk her to the back door and let her out. "I'm still that age inside."

"Me too." She steps outside. "Let me know if you're swamped. If I can, I'll come over and wait tables."

As she turns to go down the alley, I follow her and say, "Wait, I forgot to ask. Do you know anything about me having a brother or a sister?"

She stops in her tracks. Her jaw drops open. She scuffs a foot and says, "Got to go."

She hurries away, and I shake my head. What is she not telling me? If I have a sibling, why keep it a secret? I don't see a reason for all the hush hush, "Don't tell, Karina," attitudes I'm slamming up against. I'm not a fan of brick walls.

I stomp my foot in the gravel. Secrets are for other families, not ours. I thought we didn't tell lies to each other or hide the truth. At least, that's what Gigi led me to believe. But now I wonder what's going on behind my back. What else does everyone know that I don't?

Why didn't my aunt answer my question? Her reaction was certainly suspicious and fanned the flames of my curiosity. Something odd is going on, and I'm going to uncover the truth.

22

At precisely seven o'clock that morning, I turn the Closed sign around to Open and unlock the café door.

Bells on the door jingle, and Eleanor Peterson swishes in. She drops her coat on the back of a chair farthest from the door. She likes to keep an eye on the activity and sit away from the draft. She's a two-cups of coffee, one scone with jam kind of customer. For twenty-five minutes, she lingers over each morsel, and then she's off to work with a to-go cup for her job at the local refinery.

"Morning," I say, pouring her coffee. "How are you doing today?"

"Just fine, thanks."

I used to think of exchanges like this as making small talk. But Gigi told me it was a way of reaching out and connecting with another human being. Through chit chat, she said, we let the other person know they are not alone.

She said, "When you're in the café, smile and have eye contact. Exchange a few words to let them know you care. They'll leave feeling better for it. You can't tell if someone is down in the dumps from the way they look. If we can brighten even one person's life each day, we've served our purpose." She chuckled. "As well as filling hungry bellies."

I smile, reminded of my grandmother. The ache of longing for her remains, but it grows lighter each day. My routine helps keep my mind off my loss. If I didn't have to run the café, I might be sobbing in the group studio in Seattle. That wouldn't have worked for long. Making art calls for an uplifting vibe in the work setting. They might have booted me out for being a Debbie Downer.

Randy, who did me a favor by coming back for the garbage, comes in and waves to me. His work boots clomp on the hardwood floor. He's got a mop of messy brown hair. He's wearing a yellow safety vest over rust-colored overalls and a plaid flannel shirt.

He grins. "I'm here for my free coffee and scones."

I catch the twinkle in his blue eyes and smile back. He's someone I might ask out if I wasn't so busy. "Coming right up. For here or to go?"

"I'll take it to go. So did you find the stolen notebook everyone's talking about in the trash out back?"

I pour a large coffee and box up two scones and a slice

of quiche. I hand them to him with two paper napkins and a plastic fork.

Shaking my head, I say, "It wasn't in there. But thanks for giving me a chance to look. I hope if someone took it, they'll turn it in."

Randy rubs his chin. "That's too bad. Did you report it to the police?"

"Yep, and the police didn't sound hopeful. I got the feeling it's up to me to find it, which could prove to be an impossible task."

Randy smiles, and his eyes meet mine. "If anyone can find it, you will. I'd better get going. Sorry you didn't find the notebook."

"Me too. And thanks for the favor."

"See you later."

With a jingling of bells, two stooped gray-haired men in their late seventies come in and take a table for four. Mike and his friends like to sit and talk about boats.

"What'll it be, gentlemen?"

"We'll wait to order," Mike says. "Our friends will be joining us."

By eight in the morning, the place is packed. I'm buzzing around, clearing tables, pouring coffee, and bringing out plates of scones for what has become a standing-only crowd. I hope the Fire Marshall won't come in and tell me I'm over capacity. If one more person comes in and squeezes through the crowd, the windows might blow out.

In front of the café, a man in shorts and sandals with white socks up to his knees is using a metal detector. A woman digs in the flower bed. This tells me it could be the start of an ugly day. The news about the diary is bringing out the crackpots.

"Be right back," I say, and I hurry outside. "Excuse me, but this is my property. You can come in and order something. If not, I'll have to ask you to leave. Right now."

The woman scowls and sets down her trowel. "This is public property between the sidewalk and the street. I'm looking for buried treasure, and you can't stop me."

I tilt my head. She has a point. That is city property. But it is my flower bed.

"Don't you want to come in and get a bite to eat?"

She shakes her head. "I don't want someone to find it before I do." She digs under a daisy and shoves her hands in the dirt, feeling around.

I cross my arms. "Please leave the plants how you found them."

"Don't worry, I will. I just want to get the money first."

I mutter under my breath, "Me too."

The man in shorts, long socks, and sandals comes over to us.

I open my palms and say, "The idea of buried treasure is all just a rumor that's spreading around town. But it is totally unsubstantiated. All I know is Gigi's diary is gone, and I want to find it."

The man says, "Mabel, I'm going inside for a cuppa. Care to join me?"

She glares. "No, I don't. I have work to do."

I stride inside. The man follows me and leaves his metal detector by the coat rack. He waves to Mike the boater and pulls up a chair at his table. I bring him a cup and pour coffee, refilling for the others. I hope I have enough beans to last the day. At this rate, we'll be out of caffeine by noon. I text my aunt and ask her to run an errand for me. Buy three large bags of dark roast, whole bean coffee, please.

Mike the boater stands and cups his hands.

Cutting through the din in the room, he says in a loud voice, "Karina, tell us about the mystery that's going on. Or are you trying to keep it private?"

My face heats. It's a little late for that now, with the crowd eyeing me and hearing what he said. Besides, privacy is a notion for city life. You can forget about it in a place like Millersville. With all the attention focused on me, I might as well be under a microscope.

Myrtle, an older woman in a corner, cackles. "Like anything is a secret in this town. We all know each other's business."

Everyone laughs and starts talking at once.

My stomach knots. How much should I share? If I offer the truth, will they help me solve the mystery?

People stare at me, and I scan their faces, hoping to identify my unknown sibling. I wish I knew who it was. I would welcome a brother or a sister. What I'd like is if I had a secret sister who was a powerful woman around my age or maybe a bit older. Discovering a sister would be a gift, after losing Gigi. But of course, the world doesn't dish out surprises like that. We don't always get what we want. I've learned that the hard way.

I mosey through the room and make my way to Myrtle. "Okay if I use your chair?"

"Sure thing."

I stand on the chair and clap my hands to get their attention. "Hi everyone, as you all know, my grandmother passed away recently."

People murmur and look down, studying the worn floorboards.

"I haven't had time to sort through her papers. But the other day, there was a family in the dining room, and they found Gigi's journal."

Mike says, "We heard Wanda Robinson found it on Thursday."

"That's right," Myrtle says, nodding.

I say, "Actually, it was Boots Brinker who pulled it from a dining room drawer on Friday. I want to make sure we keep the facts straight."

A collective gasp goes through the group.

Someone says, "Why would she go through a drawer with personal possessions?"

I shrug. "It's partly my fault. I was running around,

because we had an overflow crowd. And I seated a family in what is usually a private part of the house."

People nod.

"And, in their defense, the Brinkers had to wait a long time to get served. My wait staff help left during the rush."

"That'd be my daughter," Aunt Jean says from the doorway.

I wave to her as she brings in bags of coffee. The smell fills the café, and it feels like everyone pauses to take a deep breath, inhaling hints of a robust, hearty blend.

"Getting back to the diary," Mike says. "Why's it so important to you?"

I decide not to tell them about the mention of the hidden money that I saw in the diary before Boots took the notebook back. Word of the potential treasure would drive the town into a frenzied froth. Everyone would want to seize the loot, which may or may not turn out to be real. The worst of it is, this all could be an imaginary game, concocted by Gigi for my entertainment. Knowing my grandmother's offbeat sense of humor, the reward for solving the riddle might be a plastic trinket buried in the back yard.

I say, "The diary is important to me because it was my grandmother's. I hope I'll learn more about her by reading it. But the most important part of why I want it is that she asked me to read it on the last night she was alive. Those were the last words she uttered before she passed away."

Mike, Myrtle, and Aunt Jean nod.

Others whisper and look down at the floor.

"All that makes sense to me," Mike says. "How can we help you get it back?"

"Yes," Myrtle says. "We need to help her."

"I'm looking for a man who was here when the diary disappeared. People said he was in his early to mid-thirties. He was wearing a newsboy cap and a green raincoat. Does that sound like anyone you know?"

They shake their heads.

"If you see a guy like that, I'd like to speak with him. Also, a page was ripped out of the journal and left on the sidewalk. Mr. Frackus found it on Friday afternoon."

Myrtle says, "What did the journal look like?"

"It has a red leather cover, and it's about this big." I hold up my hands to show the size. "I know this may sound like a stupid question, but does anyone know where it is? Or who took it?"

They look at each other and shrug.

Mike says, "I don't know."

"I have no idea," the man in shorts, white socks and sandals says. "That's why I was looking for it."

The door opens, and the flower bed digger comes in with dirt on her hands. She looks around and eyes the assembled group. She mutters, "Just going to the restroom to wash my hands."

While she goes down the hall, I glance outside at my flowerbed. She left clumps of dirt on the sidewalk. She'd better clean it up before she leaves.

"We'll organize into groups," Mike says.

Myrtle chimes in, "We'll check the public trash cans."

"That's a great idea," I say, giving her a thumbs up.

"We should all wear disposable gloves," Myrtle says, "and be careful. Don't get cut on sharp edges. I'll ask the Citizens' Auxiliary Patrol to help."

I cup my hands and say, "Thank you for looking for it, and let me know if you find it. That's all."

I hop down from the chair, and people line up to pay. They stream out the door. I thank each person for their concern and hope they'll come up with a clue or the actual item. Mike and his boating friend bus their cups and plates to a plastic bin. Myrtle wipes down tables. My aunt disappears into the kitchen with the sacks of fragrant coffee beans.

Heaving a sigh of relief, I'm grateful my customers are banding together and will conduct a search. Somewhere in town, someone knows more than they are letting on. I want to track them down before Ned the reporter pounces on them. She'd splat whatever I don't know all over the latest online edition of the paper and possibly embarrass me in the process. Although I don't know what they are, I must keep Gigi's secrets safe and protect her reputation from scandal. The diary will tell me the whole story, I hope.

23

T hat evening, I leave the house for a walk. The smell of salt air wafting off Cedar Channel draws me down to the water. A broad expanse of sandy beach is littered with seaweed, kelp whips, and driftwood. Little waves lap at the shore. Low tide gives off a fetid stench. But the tide is about to turn. High tide is on the way and will cover the odors.

I screw up my face. I landed at a low tide mark after Gigi passed away. My high tide must be coming in and bringing changes. Things have got to get better. I just have to hang in there, gut out the difficulties, and pounce on the culprit who took the diary.

Picking up a flat stone, I throw it, skipping it three times. Across the water on Cedar Island, a light in a cabin flickers. I arch an eyebrow, realizing Gigi's journal may have been hustled out of town. I should not assume that I'll find it in Millersville.

A man waves to me on the beach and walks over. It's Shane.

"What are you doing here?" I say. "And where's Lydia? I'm surprised to see you without her."

He shoves his hands in his pockets. "Lydia is being Lydia, so I needed to take a walk by myself. She's excited about working for Mr. Brinker. I guess she nailed the job interview."

"What? She didn't let me know. And she told you? I'll need to hire someone to cover for her. It's tough to find reliable help these days. When does she start the new job?"

I clamp my mouth shut. I'm blabbing because I'm rattled to my core by Lydia's abandonment. Events like this have a way of flinging me back to when I learned my parents died. My shoulders shuddered and shook, and I sobbed for hours. There was no solace in Millersville that night or for many, many weeks, and months to come. Even now, the idea of ice cream turns my stomach. It's a dessert tainted with guilt from the past. If not for my begging and pleading last request, my mom and dad would be alive.

Shane says, "I'm not sure when she starts. You'll have to ask her."

He gazes at me long enough to make me remember what dating him was like. Those eyes could take me anywhere and tell me stories without a word being said.

"Is everything all right between us?" he says. "You seem tense or distracted when I'm around."

"I'm just tapped out from working so much and, on top of that, searching for the journal. And to be honest, I think Lydia is way too young for you. Don't you want to date someone your own age? Someone with similar experiences and who's old enough to legally drink, for instance?"

He nods. "I knew the age difference bothered you. And the fact that she's your younger cousin. Is that right?"

I nudge his elbow. "Good for you, you figured it out. Now you're a detective."

"Say, if I was interested in going out with you, would you be open to that? Assuming Lydia and I were finished, that is."

"Whoa," I take a few steps back. "First of all, it would be mean to my cousin if you broke up with her, and we ended up going out. I don't want to hurt her feelings, and I don't have much family left. I don't want her angry with me. It would break girl code."

"But would you consider it?"

I put my hands on my hips. "No, I wouldn't."

"Under any circumstances?"

I poke him in the chest with my finger. "The only way that might work, and I say might because I'm not interested, is if she broke up with you first. But that'll never happen. She's head over heels infatuated with you. And

I'm too busy to date now anyway. If I did, I might pick someone else."

"Like Randy?"

I snort. There are no secrets in this town. "Yes, like Randy. He's a great guy and easy on the eyes."

"But that would be a conflict of interest, wouldn't it? Going out with one of your customers?" His lips turn up in a slight smile.

I chuckle. "Very funny, wise guy."

Without saying a word, we turn and head in the direction of my house. It's like when we were in high school and would go to the beach.

At my house, I go up a step, so we're eye to eye.

Pointing at him, I say, "Whatever you do, don't break Lydia's heart. If you do, I'll never speak with you again."

He flinches and turns to leave. "I wouldn't do that. See you around."

I use my new key to let myself in and toss my jacket on the back of a chair. I've got quiche crusts to bake and scone dough to make before I go to bed at eight tonight. I'm beat, but the work doesn't stop. Gigi said lazy people don't own thriving cafes, and she proved it to me daily.

I tie my apron strings around my waist, eyeing the window latch that is wonky and doesn't work. I need to replace it. Tomorrow after closing, I'll go to Brandon's Hardware store. Better yet, I'll ask Bernard Frackus to go out and get a latch. He seems like the type who would enjoy doing an errand as a favor for his girlfriend's grand-daughter.

I shake my head, still wrapping my mind around their secret love affair. But as the hours tick by, it becomes more real to me and believable. And he is a nice guy and decent company.

He mentioned he stays up late and watches the news at night, so I send him a text with the request.

He pings right back. "Glad to do it. See you tomorrow."

My hands are covered with flour a half hour later when the doorbell rings.

I hurry to the front door and look out before opening it. I'm not taking any chances with my safety, as a woman living alone.

A woman in her sixties stands on the front porch. She has two long gray braids, and she is holding a silver bowl. She takes out a tiny mallet, striking the metal bowl twice.

A ringing vibration comes through the window glass in the door loud and clear.

She smiles, shows her teeth, and hits the bowl again.

I frown. "What do you want?"

"Where is the money?" she says.

I shrug. "I don't know. You tell me. There might not be any. It could be a wild story someone made up."

She sticks her fingers in the mail slot and rattles it, making it clank up and down.

My chest tightens. My muscles tense. I must find a way

to live in this creaking old house without my grandmother and feel safe.

"Stop that," I say, slapping the mail slot shut.

I run upstairs, grab the baseball bat from my bedroom, and run down the steps. I brandish the bat in front of the door. "You'd better leave, or I'll call the cops."

She shrugs. "Whatever."

She clomps down the steps to a man on the sidewalk.

He stands under a streetlight with an open book in his hands. His lips are moving, like he is reading aloud. They move off down the sidewalk together.

I shake my head and double-check that the door is deadbolted.

The crackpots have come to town, and I'm not letting them in my house.

24

The next day, I sit in bed and meditate first thing in the morning. When I open my eyes, I imagine finding a way to talk with Bill Rafferty. Gigi must have wanted to meet with him, but she didn't follow through because of her illness. She'd want me to do it for her. I nod and decide to speak to him. I'm following my grandmother's clues the best I can, but she didn't give me much to go on. Except for the journal, which I lost. If only I hadn't been so careless with it. I assumed it would be on the table at the end of the day. How naïve was that? Having lived in the city, I knew better. You protect what is precious to you. You guard it from theft.

I hurry downstairs, ready to prove myself and get ready for the café to open. At seven, I dial Bill Rafferty's number. I figure a pawn broker might get up early to open his shop. I also want to get the call over with.

I tap my toes. It rings three times before a man answers. "Lo? Who's this?"

My knees tremble. "My name is Karina Walker, and I'm Gigi's granddaughter. The one who owned Gigi's Café? I'm the new owner."

"I heard she passed away. My condolences."

My palms are slick, gripping the phone. "Gigi had your phone number, and I have some questions for you. I'd like to meet with you."

"I've got a busy week. Again, my condolences."

I clear my throat. "This will just take five or ten minutes of your time."

He coughs. "This is a private number, and I'm expecting an important call."

He hangs up.

Blowing out a shaky breath, I set the phone on the kitchen counter. What did I expect, a pity party? He sounded like he was covering something up, but his tone had a hint of compassion. I'm curious, confused, and uncomfortable after speaking with him.

A familiar ache for my parents catches in my throat. I have nothing left to lose if I call him again. Those most dear to me have died. I want to talk with him and find out what he knows about Gigi and her journal. And, if I'm lucky, he might know the identity of my secret sibling.

I call him back and say as soon as he picks up, "I'd really like to meet with you."

"Why would I do that? I've got a business to run. I don't have time to chat with a café owner."

My cheeks heat. Will my body be the next one washed up on an isolated beach? Will he have his henchmen carry me off to Cedar Island and lock me in an underground cell in an abandoned detention center? I shake my head. My imagination is getting carried away. Ned broke that story in the news and won accolades for it. But that kind of thing is all in the past. No one will hurt others or hold former employees in locked cells underground like Chaos Biotechnology did. Or will they?

My mind clears, and I realize he's on the line, waiting. I have my chance, and I must take it.

I say, "Please, just meet with me for a few minutes as a favor to my grandmother?"

"Fine," he says, "I'll meet with you. I'll see you at Smithy's Pump House at five today." With a click, he hangs up.

All day, I rehearse what I'm going to say. I glance at the clock every few minutes and check the time. The café is crowded, more so than it would be on a normal day. People stop me as I hurry through the room to ask how I'm doing and if I have found my grandmother's diary.

I shake my head and thank them for their concern. "No, not yet. I hope we locate it soon."

At one o'clock, only one lonely scone remains. I hustle

into the kitchen and pre-heat the stove. Pulling scone dough wedges from the frig, I pop them onto baking sheets and into the oven.

When I bring out a batch of warm, fresh scones, people order more. It seems Gigi's journal is good for business. It would be just like her to cook up a publicity stunt to help me bring in more money and pay off my student debt.

I frown. Having the loan payments hanging over my head keeps me up at night. Majoring in art wasn't the best business decision, but I was following my heart. If only I could find a way to pay off the debt. Then I'd be carefree, and I'd sleep better.

If I knew who my mysterious sibling was, and if they existed, I'd have less on my mind. That thought gnaws at the back of my mind before dawn. Who is he or she? And where do they live? Do we have similar interests? I must find out. I'll tackle that topic when I have Gigi's diary back in my hands. One mystery to solve at a time, please. I have a limited bandwidth. I'm an artist and a restaurant owner, not a detective.

I scan the room, checking for empty coffee cups. I'm surprised anyone but me cares about Gigi's diary. But there is a whiff of promise in the air related to the purported hidden treasure. I'm motivated to read what she wrote because she was the one who raised me. What did she write that she wanted me to read? A hunger for truth burns in my belly, and I'm beyond eager to uncover her secrets.

Our head librarian, Mr. Rasmus, slides into a seat at a two-top where two people just left. While I wipe down the table with a damp cloth and pick up empty cups, he orders coffee and a scone. His plaid shirt looks fresh from the cleaners, and his brown hair is cut above the ears.

"Be right back," I say.

I buzz over to the scones, use metal tongs to set one on a plate with a pat of butter and grab a fresh, clean cup. I take the coffee pot to refill coffees.

I set his order down and pour him a cup of hot black coffee. After I make the rounds, I'll start another pot brewing.

"Cream?"

He says, "No, thanks. I'm all set."

I tilt my head. "I'd like to ask you something, because you know everyone in town."

He smiles. "Go ahead, shoot."

I set the coffee pot on the table. "Why is everyone so interested in my grandmother's diary? Doesn't it seem strange? It's a notebook filled with her thoughts. It shouldn't attract people's curiosity like it has. It's just a family matter. Don't you think?"

He nods and wraps his fingers around the white cup. "It is the buzz about town. I think the interest is due to several factors. People feel sorry for you, running this place all by yourself. Your grandmother was an icon, and we loved her."

I swallow and stay quiet, listening for what else he might say.

"And, frankly," he chuckles, holding up his hands, "we are just plain nosy about our neighbors and intrigued by the idea of a possible treasure. Any ripple in town generates a tidal wave of interest. It is out of proportion, you're right, but it'll settle down in time."

He slurps his coffee and sits back after his long speech.

I nod and pick up the coffee pot. "Thanks, that helps. I guess I forgot what small-town life was like."

"You must miss the city," he says, picking up the scone.

"Yeah, I do at times. Well, I'll let you eat and go check on the others. Thanks."

Three guests in their early sixties are speaking in hushed tones at a table.

Bernice, who runs the local escrow company, says to her friends, "I hope we find the money first. It would really help Jacklyn."

Fred, who is an attorney, taps the table. He settled my grandmother's estate.

He says. "We'd have to turn the money over to Karina if we find it."

Mary, who I admire because she is a gifted painter of landscapes, massages her temples.

I hold up the coffee pot and clear my throat. They look

at me with wide eyes, as if I have caught them discussing something clandestine. It seems everyone has secrets, even my grandmother.

Gigi was friends with Jacklyn, who owned the garden store. They spent hours talking about gardening together. I glance outside at the lumpy flower bed. I need to get out there and weed, but I haven't found time.

I refill their coffee cups. "Are you talking about the supposed buried treasure, like everyone else is? I'm not sure it exists, by the way. I didn't have a chance to examine the journal before it disappeared."

Mary says, "I guess the whole town is in on it."

Before I move away to another table, I say, "It might've been a figment of my grandmother's imagination. But she did like to make up puzzles with clues. For all I know, she may have hidden a bag of lemon drops."

They chuckle, and I move on to check other tables. I don't want treasure hunters showing up at the café when it is closed. I wipe my brow. What a pain in the butt this has turned out to be. But on the other hand, the cash register is full, and I've been swiping credit cards with my Square device attached to my smart phone. I look up and send thanks to Gigi for creating a stir from beyond the grave and bringing in money.

The day drags on. When I glance at the wall clock, the hands seem to barely move. I'm out of scones, but it is almost closing time. I go back to the kitchen and load the dishwasher.

Bells jingle on the front door, telling me a customer has come in. The door closes with a thump. Drying my hands on a dish towel, I stride out to the empty café.

Dusty Stone leans against the counter. He's over six feet tall and has a lantern jaw. A spray of freckles covers his cheeks.

He says, "I'd like a large black coffee and two scones to go."

"We're out of scones. How about a piece of quiche instead?"

A vein throbs in his forehead. He says, "I wanted a scone. Isn't that what Gigi's is known for?"

Dusty is older than me, and I didn't know him well. But Gigi said she suspected a river of anger ran through him. He slammed his fist on a table one day when she ran out of jam.

I glance at the clock. "It's almost four, which is closing time. We're sold out. I'll have more tomorrow."

He eyes me up and down. "Maybe you should have made more."

I shrug. I won't let him intimidate me, even though he is looming over me. "What can I say, we had a record crowd. Scones were flying out the door."

My mouth forms a thin line. If I was in Seattle, I'd be preparing to sell my pottery and paintings at The Wooden Boat Festival instead of dealing with this jerk. I tap my foot.

His hand clenches on the counter. His jaw is set. Man, this guy is wired tight.

He says, "I'll take the coffee then. And would you like to go out sometime?"

I take a slow, measured breath. We have nothing in common, as far as I know. And I don't feel the slightest bit interested. But I don't want to offend a guest.

The café is empty. A car drives by out front. Something about the way he is looking at me creeps me out. It dawns on me that I am alone in the building with him. A shiver runs through me, and I rub my arms. I wish I had my big, fat, heavy wooden rolling pin nearby as a weapon, just in case, or better yet, the baseball bat.

I shake my head. "I'll pass. I've got a lot going on these days. No time for fun."

When I hand him the coffee to go, he stares at me a little too long for my liking.

He says, "Your loss." He slaps two dollars down on the counter.

"It's actually three dollars," I say.

He pulls out a five and leaves it. "Keep the change. It sounds like you need it."

Slipping the cash in my apron pocket, I walk to the door and hold it open. "I have to close now. Enjoy your coffee."

"You don't have time to stand around and talk. Is that right?"

Gripping the cold doorknob, I say, "Not today, I've got to meet someone."

He glances around the deserted café and glares.

A chill runs up my spine. I step outside to be closer to other people who might help me if he blows up at me, like it feels he might, or if he makes an unwanted move. The temperature is cool for April. Briny air comes off Cedar Channel, bringing the smell of the Salish Sea.

I say in a firm voice, "Goodbye."

He stomps outside and climbs into a beat-up white pickup parked on the street.

I go inside and lock the door, turning the sign to indicate we're closed. My hands tremble. I lean back against the door and let out a breath. Gigi was right. Dusty gives off angry energy. I hope that's the last I'll see of him, but I have a feeling that won't be the case.

I think of my next task. My stomach churns, and I rest a hand on it. It's time to meet Bill Rafferty and ask some questions. I must be brave for my grandmother's sake. He might have answers that will help me solve the riddles she left behind.

25

I run upstairs to my bedroom and put on jeans and a clean sweatshirt. I slam the door on the way out and lock it. Climbing in my car, I text Bernard Frackus. Someone needs to know where I'm going. I might be paranoid, and I do have an active imagination, but I might as well play it safe.

"I'm meeting Bill Rafferty at Smithy's Pump House at five. Just letting you know in case something bad happens to me."

I head out and stop at a red light. My fingers tap the wheel. Glancing in the rear-view mirror, I bite my lip. Driving the car behind me is Ned, the reporter. She's checking her teeth in the rearview mirror. This is not a time I want her on my tail.

Even though it will make me late, I turn away from my destination. I creep into an alley near the marina. The tires crunch on gravel.

I hunch over, so Ned won't see me, and turn off the ignition. The engine pings. I wait.

Minutes later, Ned drives past in her green sedan. She's heading toward the channel, which is in the opposite direction of Smithy's.

I start the car and floor it into town. My pulse picks up. My hands are damp. Gripping the steering wheel, I wonder what I'll learn, if anything, from Bill Rafferty.

I find a parking spot on the street and stride a block to the bar. A green canvas awning with white letters covers the entrance. My phone says I'm ten minutes late. There's a text from Bernard Frackus, but I don't have time to stop and read it.

I open the heavy front door and scan the room. I didn't ask for a description of what he looked like when we were on the phone. People are chatting in booths. A few men sit on bar stools with their elbows on the counter.

I slide onto a bar stool next to a man in his sixties with a gray beard. He's the image of who I imagine Mr. Rafferty might look like.

I turn to him and say, "Are you Bill?"

"I'm not, but I can be." He winks.

I pull away from him and glance around. A man in his fifties looks up from a newspaper. He is sitting in a red leather corner booth. He takes off wire bifocals and motions for me to come over.

For some reason I'm nervous as I make my way to the booth.

He's clean-shaven, maybe in his early seventies, and he has a tan. He looks like he has been on vacation. Palm Springs is my guess. A thick gold chain around his neck peeks out from under a black polo shirt. Muscles beyond muscles bulge from the sleeves. For a guy his age, he's ripped.

"You're late," he says. "I've got another appointment in fifteen minutes. What did you want to ask me?"

I sit down and lace my fingers together in front of me to stop from fidgeting.

"I found your phone number in my grandmother's things. How did you know her?"

He plays with his reading glasses, sliding them in a circle on the table. "From the café. Everybody in town knew Gigi. And I was sorry to hear about your parents' deaths. Even though your dad was a cop, he was a good guy." He says to a man in the next booth, "Isn't that right, Scottie?"

Scottie is an even more muscly man. He is eating a meatball sandwich. With his mouth full, he nods and swallows. "That's right, boss."

Bill frowns. "I was doing time when they died."

I lean in to listen. "How did you know my parents?"

He shrugs. "I might as well tell you. Your dad was a cop, and he was interested in how I ran my business. I wasn't doing anything illegal, just selling goods in my pawn shop. Isn't that right, Scottie?"

Scottie takes a swig of beer and sets down the bottle. "That's right."

I tap the table and wait for what he might say next.

He says, "Your grandma took you in, didn't she? Did you find the money I gave her? She said she'd hide it for you until you were old enough to use it wisely."

My eyebrows shoot up. "She never mentioned that. This is the first I've heard about it."

He cocks his head. "I heard about a little girl who needed help. I'm not heartless. It was the right thing to do, to help a neighbor who was an orphan like I was."

I say, "I'm sorry to hear that. That was kind of you, but I haven't found the money yet. The clues might be in Gigi's diary. The problem is, it disappeared, and I can't find it. Do you have any idea where it might be?"

He shakes his head. "I don't, but I can help you look for it." He taps his chest and smiles. "Who knows everyone? Who has connections in and around town?"

Scottie pipes up. "You do, boss."

He nods and leans in. "And another thing. I know about your secret sister."

My mouth drops open. I have a sister? "How do you know about that?"

He shrugs. "I keep an eye on everything that goes on in town to protect my interests. I asked Gigi, and she confirmed it. I bet you'll read about it in her diary."

I gulp. "Are you sure I have a sister? Who is she and where does she live?"

He wiggles a finger in his ear. "All I can say is your sister is an important person in town. It would be in your best interests to stay on her good side."

I tilt my head. "Is she the mayor?"

He shakes his head. "No, and let's stop playing the endless guessing game. Gigi wanted you to find it out by reading her diary. She made me promise never to tell you who it is. So, I can't. I'm bound by a promise I made. And I keep my word."

"You act like you knew Gigi well, but it's obvious everyone did. I haven't seen you in the café before."

He rubs his forehead. "I do my best to stay out of sight, except for coming in this place." He grins. "My aim is to be invisible. I'm like the wind. I'm everywhere. I leave no trace behind."

I whoosh out a breath, This is all too weird. I think of everyone I know. I run through a list of names in my mind, trying to guess the identity of my sister.

Bill whispers to Scottie, "Can you believe Karina didn't know she had a sister?"

Scottie laughs.

Then it comes to me. I hold up an index finger and say, "Is it Violet? I bet it is."

I can't read the expression on his face to see if my guess was right. Before Bill answers, the door opens, and he looks toward the entrance. A cool breeze blows past. Out of habit, I turn to see who is coming in.

A man in a trench coat and a gray brimmed hat pulled low over his eyes walks in. He sits at the bar with his back to us and orders a beer in a hoarse voice.

Bill says, "Don't worry, I'll help you find the diary. Gigi told me she wanted you to read it. But you need to be sure to keep your doors and the windows locked from now on." He gives me a long look. "Especially the one in the kitchen, eh?"

Hairs on the back of my neck stand on end. Is he referring to my window with the broken latch? Are there any secrets left in this small town? I rub my fingertips together, craving the soothing feeling of clay between my fingers. That always calms me, no matter what is going on.

He shrugs. "I keep an eye on things around town. And I happen to have a soft spot for orphans, being one myself. My grandmother raised me."

My eyes grow wide. This explains his interest in me, in Gigi, and in the diary.

He says, "It's a club I never asked to join, but I made the best of it. Like you have. From what I hear, Gigi did a fine job raising you, and you turned out well."

I say, "Thanks. So, am I right that Violet Cleveland is my sister? Or is it someone else?"

He stares at the table. "It is not for me to say." He looks up at me. "I promised your grandmother I wouldn't tell you. She wanted you to read her dairy. The answers are in the pages."

My hands grow cold, and I rub them together. "Well, I don't have it, and I wish you'd make an exception for me, just this one time, and tell me."

He moves his hand as if sweeping away the idiotic request. "If I made an exception every time someone like you asked me, I'd have given away all my favors and be a broken man with no self-respect. Sorry, but I keep my word."

I sigh. "I understand. I like to keep my word too."

He smiles. "See, we have more in common that I thought, when you first called. We understand each other, orphan to orphan. Am I right?"

I shrug. He won't give up the information, so that means I've got to recover the diary if I want to learn if I have a sister, and who she is, and if Gigi hid a cache of money for me to find. "I guess. Sure, that's right."

He nods. "So, we're on the same page."

I grip the table edge. "I wonder if you can help me find someone. I'm looking for a man who wears a green raincoat and a newsboy cap. He was at the cafe when the diary went missing. Do you know who that is?"

"I might be able to locate him. Did the police say they couldn't do much about the case when you reported the missing journal?"

"Yes, but how did you know?"

He says, "I have a long reach with the law."

A woman comes over and stands by my bench seat, blocking me in. I look up and see Ned, the reporter.

She says, "Hi, Karina. I was trying to follow you but got lost. Who is this?"

She motions toward Bill and sits beside me, cutting off my exit. She pulls out a notebook. She sets her phone on the table and says to Bill, "My name is Ned, and I'm a reporter. I'm writing about the missing diary as a local interest story. What is your name, sir?"

"That, my dear, is none of your business."

I elbow her and say in a low voice, "This isn't a good time. You should leave. I'll see you later."

Bill taps his middle finger on the newspaper, as if in a warning.

Ned says, "All right if I record this conversation?"

I cringe. She has no idea who she's dealing with. If my instincts are right, this man is powerful and connected with everyone in town.

"Listen, sweetheart," Bill says, getting up. "I don't talk to reporters. Don't write about me and don't quote me." He walks into the back room and pulls a black curtain over the opening behind him.

Ned says, "Who was he? I didn't catch his name."

My pulse thumps. "No one who matters," I say, feigning nonchalance.

The man at the bar turns around and takes off his hat. It's Bernard Frackus.

I break into a broad smile and gesture for him to join us. "Good to see you. I'm glad you're here."

He slides into Bill's vacant seat opposite me. "Did you learn anything?"

26

I squirm in my seat in the red vinyl booth at Smithy's Pumphouse, clear my throat, and don't answer Mr. Frackus right away. I don't want Ned to hear what Bill Rafferty told me about my having a sister. I'm shocked and need to absorb the news when I'm alone. Bill made it sound like my sister lives in the area. I want to track her down before Ned and the whole town finds out and spreads my family secret.

"It was a dead end," I say with a shrug.

I cross my fingers under the table, where Ned and Bernard can't see. I feel bad about lying to him, but I've got to protect my best interests. I'll tell him later when Ned isn't around. It is grating on my nerves how she scribbles every comment down in her notepad. I was fine with the way she acts before, when I wasn't the focus of a pending news story. I was just the one serving her and

Violet coffee in the café. But now that her reporter's lens is fixed on me, I want to escape the limelight.

Bernard Frackus tilts his head, looking puzzled. "Are you sure?"

I nod. "But it sounded like he knew my grandmother pretty well. And he's going to help and see if he can find the man in the newsboy cap and a green rain jacket."

Ned is scribbling notes.

I rest a hand on her arm. "Could we make this off the record and not for publication? I worry that if you write about this, I'll lose the chance to find key suspects and talk to them. People will leave town or hide."

She says, "How about I'll just take notes for background?"

"Please, put it away. I trust Bernard, and we're working together. But I want to keep it a tight group for now. I don't want it splashed all over the papers."

Ned pockets her pad.

I say, "And would you please turn the recording off?"

She taps her phone to stop recording. "Why do you trust Bernard? How do you know each other? Are you related?"

He says, "I was Gigi's good friend, but Karina didn't know that."

Ned says, "This is interesting. Your grandmother was friends with Bernard, but you didn't know?"

"I had no idea. It turns out my grandmother was good at keeping secrets."

I sit back and blow out a breath. I'll talk to Bernard later, about my conversation with Bill. I'm glad she shoved her notepad in her pocket. I don't like having to watch every word I utter.

I say, "But what I do know is that until I have the journal locked back up in my house, we can't trust anyone. Many people might have it."

Ned raises an eyebrow. Her hand reaches for her pocket. The notepad comes out.

I say, "You know what, let's get out of here. I have other leads to follow up on."

Scottie in the next booth fiddles with his phone. I'm sure he's listening and will report back to his boss. For all I know, Scottie is recording us.

Bill Rafferty peers out from the back, parting the curtains, and winks at me. I nod to him. I'm grateful he agreed to look for the guy who came in and who no one has identified. I need all the help I can get.

Mr. Frackus gets up. "Good idea."

Outside, Ned says, "Where are we going?"

I look around to see if anyone is standing nearby listening. My search for the diary is making me paranoid. The sooner I resolve this, the better.

"You're not going anywhere," I say. "I really don't want you following me around. I've got a load of work to do, and I need to get started on it right away."

Ned frowns. "Fine, whatever you say." She walks off

and turns to me as she gets in her green sedan. "But I'm not going to let go of this story. This isn't the end of it."

I say to Bernard, "Come over to my place. We'll meet in the kitchen."

He nods, and we part ways. Driving to my house, I decide I need to ramp up my security system and get a video doorbell. I feel the need for extra protection after hearing Bill's warnings. In my mind, with every creak and groan of the house, I imagine someone is creeping around my home. A shadow cast by a tall tree becomes an intruder approaching. I'm saturated with fear, and that is not a way to live.

My stomach knots. My guardian, the bedrock of my beginnings, is gone. The house is empty, and I don't even have a boyfriend to hang out with.

I pull up to my house and see my ex, Jeff, standing at my back door. It looks like he is thumbing a text. My phone dings.

Getting out of the car, I see Jeff texted me.

His face is flushed. "What's going on? Did Ned find the journal yet?"

The last thing I want is for him is to listen to my conversation with Bernard. I need to send him on an errand and get him away from here while Bernard and I talk. "No, she didn't."

He looks crestfallen. "I'll help you search for it."

Before unlocking the back door, I stop. I can't let him in. His idea of a perfect world is hanging out, drinking coffee with a splash of rum, and drumming all day. I'd like an easy life like that, but I have to work, which I'll do tonight to prepare for tomorrow's crowd. But first, I want to draw up a plan to locate Gigi's notebook. Jeff would be a distraction during a meeting and a blabbermouth later on.

"You know what would help me?" I say. "If you drove to Burlington and picked up two security video doorbells. And surveillance cameras for the side yards. I'll pay you back."

If there's anything Jeff likes better than free coffee, it's tech gadgets. He's hooked, I can see it from the gleam in his eyes.

"Gotcha, I'm on it. I know the components you need. I just installed a great system for my mom. No problem."

I give him a quick smile. "Thanks. I appreciate it."

"Better get going," he says, hurrying away.

As he drives off, Bernard comes around back.

"I figured I'd better wait until he left," he says. "This discussion is for our ears only."

Ned pops up behind him, startling toward the both of us.

She says, "I parked down the block, so no one would see me."

I groan and open the door, waving them both inside. "Listen, I want anything we say to remain confidential. We'll only talk if you agree to that, Ned, and don't publish our names."

"Do we have your word?" Bernard says. "If so, I'd like to have that recorded at the beginning of our interview."

She frowns and takes a seat at the kitchen table.

"It'll mean more time for me, tracking down sources. But it'll be worth it to see my byline in print. Let's get started."

27

W e gather around my kitchen table. I tell
Ned and Bernard about my discussion
with Bill. But I leave out the part that I may
have a sister, and she lives in town. If I can't find the
journal and read about my sibling there, I suppose I could
talk to Violet and ask her what she knows. I could be way
off base, but I'll ask her directly if she and I might be
related. It's a wild idea, but I'll start with her.

Tears clog my throat, thinking of my parents and their
early deaths. And how my mother may have birthed a
secret baby and sent it away. Who raised my sibling? And
why weren't we brought up together? I've got to find out.

I push up a cuticle. "Someone must have started
rumors," I say, "about this diary and the possibility of a
treasure. You know how rumors get started in a small
town."

Bernard scratches his chin. "I do. Rumors are why Gigi and I worked so hard to keep our relationship a secret. She was so upset when your folks died, of course, and she told anyone who would listen that the car crash wasn't your parents' fault. She had all sorts of theories, including the brake lines must have been cut. But that proved to be false. She read the police report and said her daughter wouldn't drive into a tree."

I clench my hands. "But I thought my dad was driving that night. All these years, I blamed him for the car crash."

He slowly shakes his head. "Your mother was the one behind the wheel. She drove off the road and ran into the big old oak tree on Salish Drive."

I slump in my seat. Everything I had thought about how they died is false. Tears trickle down my cheeks.

Ned is quiet, listening and watching us.

Bernard says in a soft voice, "The police suspected your mother swerved to avoid hitting a cat. A neighbor came out and said they saw their black cat crossing the road."

I rub my lips. "It sounds like something she'd do. She loved animals and especially cats. But my dad was allergic to them, so we couldn't have one."

Ned says, "Maybe you should go down to the police station and ask to see the police report, just to make sure."

I cock my head. I don't feel the need to read the report, but someday I would like to talk to a detective or an officer who worked with my dad. I'm not sure I'll find someone to talk with me, because it has been a long time since he passed away. But I tuck the idea away for later when I have more time.

Bernard says, "I saw the police report with my own eyes, and I believe what it said. I think Gigi was desperate to shift the blame away from your mother. Grief can make people say and do strange things."

I nod. Grief made me agree to her request to run the restaurant. I told her what she wanted to hear in her final hours. I'm glad it brought her peace, but moving back home has brought chaos into my life.

I say, "Right before Gigi died, she asked me to read her journal. And the weird thing is, she told Bill Rafferty she wanted me to read her diary. Doesn't that seem strange?"

Bernard says, "She knew everyone in town. I think that's why the café was so popular. Everyone wanted to be around her. She was interested in each person's story, and she was warm and caring. Coming in here was like going on vacation to a sunny beach. You'd leave feeling better."

"She was amazing," I say. "If I can live up to half of who she was, I'll be happy."

He reaches over and pats my hand. "You are doing a wonderful job running this place, Karina. You should be proud of yourself. I know Gigi would be."

In a tight voice, I say, "Thank you for saying that. Some days it feels like I stepped into the middle of a tornado."

Ned opens her notebook. "Karina, did I hear you say your grandmother told you to read the journal, and that was when she was on her death bed?"

I bite my lower lip, recalling that dark night. "Yes, she did."

She taps a pencil to her lips. "This could be a weekend feature life style story about small town living and how connected you all are. How you care for and depend on each other. Everyone is chipping in and helping you find your grandmother's journal."

I lean in. "I could see that. The only downside is it'll bring in more tourists to town."

Bernard says, "But it would give a boost to local businesses, don't you think?"

I blow out a breath. "I'm not sure I can handle any more people coming in. But it would help the other store owners, you're right."

Ned's phone rings. "I've got to take this," she says, snapping her notebook closed. "It's my boss. If you find the journal, let me know."

I walk her to the door. As she heads outside, I hear her say, "Sure, I'll get right on it. Be back in Seattle as soon as I can."

I go back to the kitchen, where Bernard is washing dishes.

I say, "I've got some things to tell you that I didn't want to say in front of Ned."

He turns off the water and leans against the counter. "Go ahead, I'm all ears."

"Bill told me he gave Gigi money for me after I was orphaned. Because he was an orphan. He also said my dad was good cop. And, he said I have a sister who lives around here. I didn't know that."

Bernard studies me. "That's a lot to absorb all at once. I suspected from a few things Gigi said that she had a secret stash of money to give you when you were old enough."

My head snaps up. "Why didn't she tell me? I could've used it to pay for college."

He tilts his head. "I think she was waiting until you were old enough, so you would spend it wisely. And then she got sick and was distracted. But don't get your hopes up too high. I don't think it is a lot of money. It might not make a major difference in your life." He waves his hands in the air. "And who knows? Like Gigi's suspicions about the brake lines being cut, it could be idle chatter. It could amount to nothing."

"I get that and totally understand," I say. "I'm motivated to find the notebook, but I'm also prepared to find a big fat nothing at the end of my search, after reading what's in the journal. But what did you make of what Bill said about my having a sister? Do you know anything you're not telling me? Do you know where I can find her?"

He shrugs. "I can't help you with that. You know as much as I do. What does your gut say?"

I'm about to answer when Jeff knocks on the back door. I let him in, and he carries bags into the kitchen, setting them on the table.

Jeff introduces himself to Bernard, and they shake hands.

"Bernard is helping me," I say to Jeff. "And he's a good friend of the family. Did you get everything?"

"I did. When we install these, you'll be able to see who's snooping around. I bought battery-powered video doorbells. We don't have to hard wire them, which makes it easier. The batteries last four months."

Bernard says, "I've been thinking about getting one of those. You never know who might be hanging around."

I give him a look and try to signal that we should be subtle and not to tell Jeff too much. If Jeff knew that Gigi left money for me, according to what Bill said, then Jeff might figure out a way to weasel in and take a share. He used to say he wanted the easy life, but he didn't want to work for it. I should have paid attention to that much earlier, before we lived together. It was a flashing red light that I drove through, ignoring the signs. When I broke up, his free ride was over. That's the last time I'll date a drummer.

We install the doorbells and mount the surveillance cameras on the sides of the house.

Tromping inside, we congratulate each other and give each other high fives.

"You made it easy," I say to Jeff. "Without you, I'd still be reading the manual."

"You're the man," Bernard says.

Jeff and I glance at each other and smile.

Bernard cracks me up when he tries to sound hip.

I heat lasagna for dinner for the three of us. It's been frozen since Gigi passed away, and it is chewy but edible. I haven't had time to do a proper grocery shop since Friday, and I'm out of salad greens or anything healthy.

Bernard eats a last bite and sets down his fork. "That was mighty good. Just don't tell my doctor about this. I didn't eat any vegetables."

Going to the freezer, I pull out a pint of rocky road ice cream and set it on the table with three spoons. "We might as well have dessert, too. This'll be our secret."

Jeff grins. "I love secrets. Karina, you're giving off a mysterious vibe, like you know something that you're not telling me."

Bernard jabs a spoon into the ice cream. "She is, isn't she? Just like her grandmother."

The air warms, as if my grandmother is here and wrapping her arms around me.

"I miss her so much. The café isn't the same without her. But I'm trying my best."

"People like your food," Bernard says. "They're coming in, aren't they, like they used to?"

"They are, but I'm not sure if it's because of rumors about my grandmother's journal, or if they want to see if I can run the place without her. Whatever the reason, I'm glad the café is busy. Gigi would be pleased about that."

Jeff gets up. "Speaking of that, I've got to run back to Seattle. Got business to attend to. The band is practicing for a gig."

"Wait, I need to pay you for what you bought." I pull cash from my purse and count it out, handing it over to him.

He leans over and brushes my cheek with a kiss. He smells of cloves, aftershave and coffee breath, a familiar combination.

Ushering him out, I say, "Thanks for running that errand and helping us install it. I really appreciate it."

"Good to see you."

"You too."

"Good luck finding your grandma's diary."

"Thanks, I need it. Hope your gig goes well."

He says, "It's at the Tractor Tavern. Come down and hear us."

I tuck my lips together and cover up a frown. As our relationship wore on, I was less and less a fan of his band. I prefer solo artists and acoustic music now, not amplified rock bands. "Sorry, but I can't. It's too busy for me to leave, even for one night."

"That's too bad," he says. "You shouldn't work so hard. You're tied to the café, just like your grandmother was. You always said you didn't want to end up that way."

I shrug. "I guess people change. I don't mind it so much. I'm getting used to it."

I wave goodbye to him and close the door, locking it.

Turning to Bernard, I say, "Jeff used to be my boyfriend, but I don't really trust him. He was fun at first. But then I realized he expected me to pay all the bills. How can you trust a drummer?"

Bernard chuckles. "Or a high school science teacher, for that matter. Tell me more about your life in the city."

28

We sit down, and I tell Bernard about my life as a potter and painter in Seattle and answer his questions. "I spent most of my time at the art studio, making pots for street fairs and galleries. To make ends meet, Jeff and I took in room-mates. The kitchen was never clean, which drove me crazy."

Bernard says, "Your grandmother prided herself in keeping a spotless house."

I rub my temples. "She did. And Jeff's constant drum-ming gave me headaches. I admired his passion for it at first, but then it didn't sound like music, just a lot of crashing and banging. He practiced at three in the morning sometimes. What about the rest of us, who were sleeping?"

He rubs his chin. "So, although you liked your career

there as an independent artist, the personal relationship part of your life was lacking?"

I arch an eyebrow. "It was definitely lacking. It was one of those things, where you fall into being friends because it's easy with jokes and laughter. But slowly, before you even notice it, the friendship turns into something else. An obligation tinged with sadness for what was lost. I think we both had expectations but didn't voice them. I wanted him to chip in and pay his way, but I didn't speak up. In hindsight, I expected him to change, and I stored up a lot of resentment. That never works, does it?"

He shakes his head. "That sounds like an unhealthy situation. Too bad you couldn't have had a heart-to-heart discussion and cleared it up."

I wipe my brow. "I think we were too far gone for that. When we met, I should have stayed friends and not let him move in with me. He made it clear from the start that he didn't want a day job, but I didn't listen or pay attention. I had this image of who he was, and I expected him to be that person. And now I realize it wouldn't have worked, no matter how much we talked about it. He is who he is. The fault is with me for thinking he was someone else."

Bernard says, "I think you're being too hard on yourself."

I shrug. "It helps to be honest with myself. If I am, then maybe I won't make the same mistakes again."

He nods. "Good for you, pointing a spotlight on your

inner life. Fortunately for me, my friendship with your grandmother went in a different direction. We went from fleeting hellos to a deep friendship and an open-hearted love. I'm lucky to have known her."

I squeeze my hands together. "She was lucky too. I'm glad she had you in her life. I just wish she would have told me about you."

He wiggles his eyebrows. "I just had a crazy thought. I'm curious about Bill Rafferty. Why don't we look him up on the internet and see if we can find anything out about him?"

I cock my head and give him a puzzled look because this is an odd turn of conversation.

"As a teacher, I'm naturally curious," he says. "I figure the more information we have, the better. In case we need to ask him for another favor."

"Sure," I say. "Why not?"

After thirty minutes of searching on my laptop, we come up with three companies associated with William Rafferty that are registered with the Secretary of State. He could own more companies registered under a different name. Bodecker Enterprises is the pawn shop he runs with the same name.

"Bodecker's looks interesting," I say. "He's president of that company."

"Let me see if he has any obvious links to the police," Bernard says. "He did tell you he had influence with law enforcement, didn't he?"

"He did." I push the laptop over to him. His fingers fly over the keyboard and soon, we read an article about Bill's trial. He spent a short time in prison. We also have a list of the Police Charity Ball's Gold Club members, for those who gave over fifty thousand dollars.

"Bingo," Bernard says, jabbing a finger at the screen. "We have Bodecker's, Dinson's and Raspberry Lane giving high-powered money to a police charity event."

I say, "But this doesn't prove anything or tell us much. Are you wondering if Bill bribed the police to look the other way on some of his nefarious dealings?"

He fiddles with the frames of his glasses. "Yes, I was thinking exactly that. I'm glad he didn't have anything to do with your parents' car accident, but we don't know what other dealings he's had with the police."

"We don't. You know, this has been a lot to accept. I'm angry at my mom for not being more careful when she was driving, and I'm angry at Gigi for not being truthful about my dad's role in the accident. I wish they'd never gone out that night."

He looks over his glasses. "Where were they going that late at night? Gigi never told me."

I bite my lower lip. "They went to a party, and it was a cold, dark night. The roads were icy. Before they left, I whined and begged for them to bring home a carton of Rocky Road ice cream. I had a sore throat, and I'd been home sick. I put up a big enough fuss that they caved. If they'd come straight home, she wouldn't have hit a tree." I whoosh out a breath and lean over. My stomach is queasy. "Do you think it's my fault they died?"

He says, "There are no simple answers to life's dilemmas. You were dealt a bad hand, and it wasn't your fault. A cat was on an icy road, by chance. You weren't responsible for that. For your own good, you need to forget about the accident. That's what I used to tell Gigi. Rehashing the event won't bring you peace."

I sigh. I know he's right, and I must let go of the blame. It was no one's fault.

He pats the table. "I'm serious. Let it go. I saw the toll it took on your grandmother. She fretted and worried over who caused the accident. It gave her stomach aches. Don't hold onto it, like she did."

"But I thought she was always happy. I had no idea."

"She felt she had to be the sunshine for you, given all the sadness you were dealing with."

I glance at the clock. It is nine at night, when I'm usually asleep after prepping for the next day. Standing, I stretch my arms.

"I've got to go to bed. I'm exhausted. I'm glad the house is secure, and we made some progress today."

He gets up. "We did. I'm very pleased. Sleep well."

My phone chimes, and I check the screen. Someone is lurking in the shadows by my front door. I turn the phone to Bernard and show him.

"Trouble, eh?" he says.

I say, "It's awful late. Should we answer it? If it is one of those treasure hunters, I'll send them away."

He holds up his hands. "We have to be cautious. But we really should see who it is."

Peering at the phone, I watch the person step closer to the door. They're tall, broad-shouldered, and wearing a dark sweatshirt with the hood pulled up. The person is looking down, and I can't see their face.

I cringe.

The new doorbell rings.

My heart thumps. No one comes to the café at this time of the night. Everyone in town knows that in order to run Gigi's, I need my sleep.

Bernard stares in the direction of the front door.

My skin prickles. "It is suspicious, someone showing up at this time of night. I'll investigate and see who it is."

He adjusts his glasses with a trembling hand.

I shrug. "Whoever is out there might know something about the journal."

"Should we arm ourselves at this time of night?" Bernard grabs a kitchen knife from the counter. "I suggest you do the same."

"I don't know if we need to go that far, but we do have to be very careful. This seems like overkill to me, but what the heck." I take a sharp paring knife. The kitchen tool fits comfortably in my hands. Better to be prepared than surprised.

"Fine, let's go," he says. "Don't let them in, no matter what."

Each footstep seems to take me forever on the long walk to the front door. The wood floor creaks under my weight. Behind me, Bernard makes the floorboards groan.

Who is waiting outside, and why are they here? What do they want?

I suddenly have the urge to go to the bathroom as my nerves are reaching overload. I hope it is not a home invader, ringing the bell to see if anyone is home. I wish for a time when the most difficult part of a day was waking up before dawn to bake scones. How little I appreciated my simple life. When all this is over, I'm going to make an effort to complain less.

I glance at the doorbell camera before going to the door, where I'll be seen by whoever is outside. A tall, hooded man is at my front door. All I can hear is the pounding of my heart.

After confronting Bill Rafferty, I'm on edge. If I have to use the knife, I hope it won't be turned around and thrust into my soft flesh.

Gripping the knife, I peer out. My throat is dry.

"Who is it?" I say with as much authority as I can muster.

Bernard appears by my side. "Identify yourself."

The giant pulls off the hood of his sweatshirt. He's younger than I expected, maybe in his early-thirties. He gives me a hesitant smile through the glass. Laugh lines around his eyes make him appear kind.

"I'm the man who was wearing the green raincoat and the newsboy cap. I work for Bill Rafferty, and he sent me. May I come in?"

My chest constricts. He's not wearing the rain coat or hat now. How can I be sure he is who he says he is? "Why are you here at this time of night?

My mind cooks up wild schemes for the reasons this man is on my porch. I'm sleep-deprived and stressed from recent events, and my mind is going in many different directions. For all I know, Bill may have planted listening devices in my home. That's unlikely though. I'm just a café owner, making scones and quiche, pouring gallons of coffee. There's nothing special about me or my life.

I cross my arms. If I let this man in, are we taking a big risk? He could tie us up and threaten us, or worse. He is a large, strong-looking man. He has sixty or more pounds on me, and his biceps are bulging.

I doubt Bernard and I could overpower him. Fear and lack of sleep is making my brain freak out. I must be alert to keep my promise to Gigi and read the journal.

But if I let this mysterious man into my house, I might learn more about the whereabouts of the diary. The man in the newsboy cap may be the key to the mystery. I loosen my grip around the knife. I want to settle this.

"I think we should let him in," I say to Bernard. "And get this over with. Let's find out what he knows."

"Talk to him through the glass. We'll be better off with a barrier between us."

I nod. It's a wise move. I say to the stranger, "Say whatever you want to me now, while the door is closed."

The man outside says, "I was sent to give you information about the location of the missing journal. Bill said it would interest you. He said it's the least he can do, under the unfortunate circumstances."

I shake my head. Is he spinning tales to soften me up? I whisper to Bernard, "I doubt Bill wants to help me by sending an employee over at night. Is this all a ruse to get me to open the door?"

Bill Rafferty's man says, "You have trust issues. You need to work on that." He chuckles and doesn't move. He stands his ground, looking in.

I say, "Tell me what you were sent here to say."

"Only if you let me in and give me a scone. It's the least you can do. It's chilly out here, and I promise I won't hurt you."

I hope he's not playing me. If I open the door, he might take advantage of us. But I'm probably getting carried away with my imaginings. I need to crash in bed and sleep until morning. But my wild thoughts run on. He could wipe us both out while we're vulnerable, eating baked goods in the kitchen and choking on crumbs, as a hail of bullets hit us.

"Is anyone with you?" I say.

"Nope."

Bernard says in a low voice, "Let him in. We'll pat him down first."

I say, "We'd better do that. He looks like a professional who happens to like scones. He might have a knife or a gun hidden."

"I can hear you," the hulking man on the porch says. "You're being rude. Just talk to me. And if you're going to talk *about* me, the least you can do is keep your voices down. I'm beginning to feel left out. As I said, I'm not here to harm anyone."

I want the information he has, but I don't feel comfortable letting him inside at night. "Come back in the morning when more people are around. Then, I'll feel safe. During the day, nothing bad happens."

He chuckles. "You hold onto that notion if it makes you feel better. No, we'd better do this now. My boss sent me. Your lights were on, so I knew you were awake."

Bernard says, "We have nothing to lose."

"Except our lives. And my entire business and the family home. But if we're dead, that won't matter." I rest a hand on the door handle. I'm cold and full of fear. Too much has been happening in the last few days.

I hold up a finger and say, "Hold on, I'll let someone know you're coming inside, in case you try something. What is your name, besides the man in the newsboy cap with the green raincoat?"

"Flash," he says with a toothy grin.

With trembling fingers, I text my Aunt Jean. "Flash, who works for Bill Rafferty, is coming in my kitchen for scones. Mr. Frackus is with me. In case we're maimed or murdered or disappear."

29

I unlock the deadbolt with shaking hands. I can't believe I'm letting a complete stranger into my home at night. My old high school science teacher who was my grandmother's secret boyfriend is my only back up. The street is quiet, so there'll be no help coming from others.

Opening the door, I point and say, "Stay there and don't move. I'll pat you down. I'm warning you. My partner has a weapon."

Bernard brandishes a long carving knife.

"Fine, fine." Flash raises his arms and smiles. "It's clear you two don't trust me."

Squeezing Flash's biceps, I decide he must work out every day lifting weights. He has muscles in his wrinkles. Coming to his socks, I pull out a pack of gum.

"Flavor Fresh Mint?" I say.

"My favorite."

When he smiles, something inside me thaws. But I must remain clear-headed and not be wowed or influenced by appearances and good-time Flash vibes. He probably puts on the charm for any female.

I check his other sock. "Ah hah."

Pulling out a switchblade, I toss it into the bushes. "You can retrieve that on the way out."

To Bernard, I say, "All clear."

I say to Flash, "Come inside. It's a bit late for scones, but I guess I'll make an exception in exchange for information about the diary."

I brew coffee, preheat the oven, and place scone dough wedges on baking pans. The situation is surreal. While I work, Bernard and Flash sit at the kitchen table and make small talk. My hands are jittery. I can't wait to hear what Flash knows about the diary.

I pull the scones from the oven and use a red spatula to move them to a white plate. Setting the plate before them, I say, "I'll serve you coffee, and we'll get down to business."

I hand them each a cup of black coffee. Flash looks like the kind of guy who is a late-night coffee drinker. I fill a glass of water for myself.

Bernard groans. "The scones smell good."

Flash reaches for one with a gleam in his eyes. "Makes me weak in the knees."

He munches on a scone and wipes his mouth. For

being a possible gangster, he's polite with a wicked sense of humor. He has cracked Bernard and me up several times. But we're an easy audience because of our nerves.

If he tries anything, I could threaten him with my new hand-held mixer's stainless steel turbo beaters. I had my eye on a Candy Apple Red KitchenAid model with nine speed options for some time and bought it last week. If he tries to hurt us, or steal it, he'll learn a lesson about how fierce I can be. Hands off my mixer.

The kitchen is warm, but my body is rigid. I'm wary of what I'll learn and unsure about what will be revealed.

"Enough mincing around," I say. "Let's get down to business. Or are you just here to clean me out of tomorrow's stock of scones?"

Flash says with a smile, "That's an idea. But could I just take some home to my wife? She'd like that."

Bernard pipes up. "Good idea. Keep the wife happy. While you're at it, Karina, I'd like one to go, if you have enough."

So, Flash is married. That takes those thoughts off the table. I'll have to be content with a life on my own and my Candy Red mixer, which will serve as a weapon as long its plugged in. Blades whirring, I'll tell intruders to stay back. I'm armed.

I put a hand on my hip. "It's ten at night guys. This isn't the short order café. But, fine, since you like them so much."

Setting two bags of warm scones in front of them, I sit

down, eager to find out what Flash is here to say. I start at the beginning. "What do you know about the journal?"

Flash looks down at his sneakers. They must be size twelve. "Not much."

"Tell me everything, now."

He clears his throat but stays silent.

I say, "What did your boss send you over to tell me about the missing journal?"

"He heard there's a little girl involved," Flash says. "She swiped the journal. Because it was red and caught her eye."

I say, "Are you talking about little Maddie Robinson?"

He nods.

Tapping my lips with a finger, I'm sure this isn't true. Charming, sweet Maddie wouldn't do that. She and her mother were sincere, innocent, and without a flicker of betraying a lie. I believed them when they said they had no idea where the diary was. If Maddie was acting, she deserves an award. She could be the next child star.

"I seriously doubt a little girl is the guilty party with light fingers," I say. "That's probably a story told to distract me from the real thief. I've got a lot of suspects on my list, and Maddie isn't among them. I'm looking for an adult with an ulterior motive." I give him a cold, hard stare. "Your name is on the list."

He squirms. "I didn't do anything. Scratch my name off."

Bernard says to me, "He may be right. If Flash took it,

why would he come here and talk with you? Except perhaps as a red herring."

I arch an eyebrow at Flash, who is tying his shoelace. I'm not sure what to believe anymore. Who is guilty and has the journal? It seems like lots of people could have a reason to take it. Alarm bells are going off in my head, but my gut tells me to trust this tall stranger at my kitchen table. I toss out a last question in case he's leading us down a dead end.

"Your boss may have taken the diary, to cover his tracks in case his name is mentioned in it. He knew my grandmother and spoke with her. Word has it you came into the café at the time the diary disappeared. You could've pocketed it and slipped away with no one knowing."

Flash says, "I'm sort of hard to miss at my size. And I have a young daughter. There's no way I'd jeopardize her safety and security by stealing. I'm a bodyguard and security detail for Mr. Rafferty. But I don't get actively involved in his operations."

I say to Bernard, "That's a good cover story, isn't it? Do you believe the bit about the daughter at home?"

"I do. I'm buying it."

"I guess I almost am." Turning to Flash, I say, "My gut says you're telling the truth, and I hope I don't regret trusting you. Because you must know so much about what's going on in town, will you look over our list of suspects? You could help us rule out people."

He glances at his phone. "Sure, but I only have a half hour. I need to be home to spell my wife. She's a nurse and works the night shift at the hospital. Mr. Rafferty pays okay, but with the cost of living, we both have to work."

I give him a slight smile. To my surprise, I'm warming to Flash, who is facing challenges we all confront. But I'm not entirely sold on his story.

"Let's get started."

30

H unched over the kitchen table with Flash, who we've taken into our confidence for some crazy reason, Bernard and I run through our list of suspects. A pawn broker's security detail, a retired high school science teacher and me, a potter and painter and café owner, make an unlikely team.

Pointing at my laptop screen, I say, "Kenny Robinson is a history buff. He was practically salivating over the idea of reading the journal."

Flash shrugs. "I'm not sure that's enough motivation. Snooping around reading a decades old diary doesn't sound like it'd fit with a sporting goods store owner. Who else do we have?"

Bernard says, "Boots Brinker. She's my favorite for the crime. She had the goods in her hands and denied knowing where it went. Remember, she wants to use it as part of her research for an economics paper on consumer behavior when stock markets crash, like on Black Monday."

"Wanda Robinson might have it," I say. "She's writing a novel about a missing journal. She's an improv actor and could cover up facial tells with a who-me façade. But I like her and respect her. Somehow, I doubt it's her."

Flash scratches his stubbled chin. "Was Black Monday a real thing? You mentioned it, but I've never heard of it."

"Let me see what I can find to explain it." Bernard opens the internet browser on my laptop and reads aloud, "Black Monday was on Monday, October 19, 1987, when the global stock market suffered a severe stock market crash. Headlines of the day reported *Bedlam on Wall St.* and *Wall St. Panic.*"

He clicks on a related page for the Federal Reserve history.

I take a turn reading aloud, "The Dow Jones Industrial average dropped 22.6 percent, a loss that remains the largest one-day stock market decline in history."

Flash says, "Wow. I had no idea."

I continue. "There was an asset bubble building months before."

"Sounds like a gas bubble, where you burp a baby," Flash says.

We chuckle.

I say, reading what's on the screen, "The federal government had a bigger than expected trade deficit.

Triple witching day happened on a Friday, where options and futures contracts expired. Monday morning before U.S. markets opened, stock markets in and around Asia plunged. When the U.S. market opened, everyone was selling. There were more sell orders than buyers and that created a domino effect."

Bernard reads more. "After that, regulators put new rules in place, allowing stock exchanges to temporarily halt trading if there are unusually large price drops."

Flash says, "So, it was a real event and is unlikely to repeat itself. But it makes me uncomfortable. I have stocks in my retirement plan, along with certificates of deposit. I don't want to be stuck if the stock market sours."

Bernard claps him on the back. "I'm with you, using the same strategy. I'm in both CD's and stocks. But make sure you monitor it. Now let's finish with the list so you can head home."

"I'm beginning to believe you and Bill Rafferty don't have the diary," I say. "Otherwise, you wouldn't be here. Are you hunting for it too?"

Flash's eyes grow wide. "No, we're trying to help you. Bill feels bad about you being an orphan. He knew your grandmother."

Bernard frowns. "How well did he know Gigi?"

Flash fiddles with the paper sack holding the scones for his wife and daughter. "It might be best if you talk directly with him about that."

"Let's finish going over the suspects," I say. "My aunt

and my cousin don't care about the journal. But our librarian is keen to read it."

Flash says, "Mr. Rasmus wouldn't steal it."

"Are you sure?" I say.

He nods. "It is part of my job to research and know residents and their vices."

"I wouldn't want to know everyone's secrets," I say. Glancing at Bernard, I add, "But it seems like I've been unearthing some of my own family secrets lately."

The guys nod. Flash says, "We all have them."

I say, "Okay, we only have a few more left on the list. There's Shane, who's my cousin's boyfriend."

"And you have a secret crush on him," Flash says with a smile.

My face heats. I clear my throat and study the ceiling. Is it that obvious? How embarrassing.

"I'd call him clean," Flash says. "He's an architecture student who should focus more on his studies and less on his girlfriend who is too young for him."

I stare at him. "I totally agree with you on that. It turns out you're an expert on everyone."

He shrugs. "Mr. Rafferty has me track people's interests and whereabouts. It pays to be cautious when you're in the business of lending money and selling people's possessions."

"I'll bet," I say. "So, Shane's out. My former boyfriend in Seattle, Jeff, wanted to find it. He heard it had a treasure map."

"I don't know anything about this Jeff." Flash stands and stretches his back.

"Wait a minute," Bernard says, staring at the computer screen. "What's my name doing on this list? I'm the one helping you. You shouldn't be suspicious of me."

I get up and shake out my legs, which are stiff from sitting so long. "I was developing a complete list and jotting down anyone who came to mind." I pat his back. "Please, don't be offended. I didn't want to overlook anyone with a possible motive or who was here that day."

He huffs. "This is what comes from helping a relative of my girlfriend."

"I'll take you off the list eventually. I'm sure every person on the list would be offended if they knew that I suspected them. I appreciate your help. And yours, Flash."

Flash gives me a wide smile. "Glad to help. Got to run. Thanks for the scones."

He takes the bag and heads for the door.

"Tell your wife hello from us," I call as he leaves.

I lock the front door and watch as he picks up his switchblade from the bushes.

In the kitchen, Bernard says, "Now that he's gone, I'll go home. It's been an interesting evening. Far better than watching a rerun of *Masterpiece Theatre*."

I smile. He probably also likes the show *Jeopardy*, which I secretly binge on. Gigi and I watched it together, even in the weeks leading up to her death.

"I have an idea," I say. "Let's gather the suspects in one

room and grill them as a group. We'll flush out the culprit."

He squints, as if mulling it over. "That's an unusual approach, but one I can get behind. Are you thinking we'll do it in the café?"

"Yes," I say, "in the main front room, tomorrow afternoon. Right after closing."

"Might as well give it a try. I suppose it can't hurt."

31

It's mayhem in Gigi's Café the next day. Last night I texted, called, and emailed suspects and asked them to appear at four o'clock in the café today. I said I was offering free scones and holding a mystery party. "You won't want to miss this," I said. "It will be the talk of the town, and only certain special people are invited. I'll save a seat for you. Be on time!"

Word has spread about the case of the missing journal. Guests fill the café all day. People are lined up out the door. Every seat is taken. Forks clatter. Chatter fills the front room.

I buzz around, handing out coffee, scones, and quiche. Making my rounds, I overhear gossip. People speculate about who took the journal. As I refill coffees for a couple in their sixties, the woman fingers her reading glasses on a chain around her neck.

She looks up at me and says, "I hear there will be a special meeting taking place after you close today. Why weren't we invited? I'd like to attend."

Her gray-haired husband tugs on his goatee. "We should have been included. We eat here often."

I set the coffee pot on the table. "I only invited people who were here the afternoon the diary disappeared. I couldn't include everyone. There wouldn't be space for everyone."

"Can we come and watch?" she says, glancing at her husband, who nods. "We won't take up much space. We can sit in the hall. I know, you could webcast it on Zoom or YouTube and sell tickets, like to a show."

I resist the urge to roll my eyes. "That's creative thinking, but I'm trying to keep it low key with a personal approach, so an online event is out. And I don't have enough space for more people. But I'll let you know how it goes. Come in tomorrow to get the details."

He says, "We will."

She says, "If you change your mind, I can run the webcast for you. Here's my card."

I thank her and tuck the card in my apron pocket. The rest of the day rolls by at a brisk pace with a full café. I need to hire an assistant to help me in the kitchen and waiting tables as soon as this mystery is resolved. I smile and trot around the café, handing out orders and refilling coffee cups. I'm looking forward to our event this afternoon.

But by three o'clock, I've had one too many cups of coffee. I'm shaking like my new mixer. I only have an hour left until the meeting. I hope I'll learn who stole the diary, and I'll soon be holding it in my hands.

My nerves are jangled by the time I close the front door a few minutes early and turn the open sign around to closed. I clear the last of the plates and cups from tables and load the dishwasher.

My knees shake. I wipe my brow. In ten minutes, suspects will gather around tables. I hope we'll solve the mystery. That would free up my time to track down my secret sister and work in my art studio. I'd like to paint a new scene depicting a red journal, dark tree branches, and an old house. It'll be moody and sinister, in crimson and black. I might paint a single green leaf on the walkway in front of the house for contrast.

Bells on the door jingle when Eleanor Peterson comes in after her shift at the refinery. I've asked her to come and take notes.

"Can I get you a glass of water or a cup of coffee?" I say.

She shakes her head and sits. "I'm fine. I can't wait to see what happens."

I blow out a breath. "Me too."

Mike the boater arrives. I've asked him to be the bouncer if anyone gets rowdy. He'll also record what everyone says on his phone.

I shake his hand. He's got a firm grip. "Thanks for coming. I wanted impartial witnesses."

Bernard Frackus comes in. Wind blows leaves inside before he closes the door.

"Ready?" he says, taking off a gray fedora and trench coat, hanging them on the coat rack.

Nodding, I say, "I think so. I hope whoever took it will fess up and give it back."

People file in and sit at tables.

A hush falls over the normally noisy room.

Flash, as tall as ever, slides into a seat. He takes off his green raincoat and hangs it on the back of his chair. Bill Rafferty joins him at the table for two and fingers a gold chain around his neck.

I nod to them. "Gentlemen."

When everyone is seated, I say, clapping my hands, "Okay, let's get started. I appreciate you all coming here to discuss Gigi's missing journal. I'll introduce each of you and review your possible motives. And then, I hope we'll find out who took my grandmother's diary."

I scan the group. "One of you may have it with you, even now. There will be no negative vibes or repercussions if someone hands it over now. I only want to read it and get to know my grandmother better. She asked me to read it just before she passed away. So, I know it meant a lot to her, and I want to have it back in this house where it belongs."

People murmur, "That's right."

Mr. Rafferty picks up a salt shaker, studying it. Flash looks around the room. Bernard fiddles with his glasses.

I say, "Does anyone want to hand the diary over now? We could avoid the whole meeting if that happened."

No one moves.

Mike sits, hands in his lap, watching his phone record the meeting.

Eleanor is taking notes on a yellow legal pad.

Wanda Robinson is sitting with her family, typing on her phone.

Boots Brinker and her brother yawn.

Boots's dad, Bill, says, "Let's get this over with. I've got business to attend to."

"Sure thing." I point to Flash. "This is Flash. In case anyone wondered, he's the man in the newsboy cap who was wearing a green raincoat on the day of the crime."

Flash grins and waves.

"Flash is a suspect because he came in the café right around the time the diary went missing."

Flash says, "I only stopped in for scones, because my wife likes them. But when I saw you were too busy to help me, I left."

I nod. He's right. Gigi would scold me for missing a chance to serve a guest. But Lydia had stepped out, and I was short staffed at the time.

"Sitting at the same table is Bill Rafferty, his boss."

I stop myself from mentioning my parents' car crash. I've got to accept it was an accident. No one ordered their deaths or cut the brake lines. My folks are gone, and I was lucky enough to be raised by my amazing, incredible grandmother.

"I suspected Mr. Rafferty, and I thought he had Flash steal the diary. For all I know, your name might be mentioned in the journal entries."

Bill Rafferty stands and clear his throat. "The diary only has meaning to you, Karina. There's no reason I would steal something of sentimental value. I enjoyed talking with Gigi, but I wouldn't violate her privacy and take her diary. That's not my style. What would I do with it?"

He plunks down in his seat and gives me a tender, grandfatherly gaze.

He says, "And I wasn't in town that day. I was in Wenatchee arranging for a shipment of Red Delicious apples."

I screw up my face because that sounds phony. It's April. Apples won't be ripe for months. Besides, he could've called or emailed to arrange a delivery, instead of driving over there. Why would he want a shipment of apples anyway? He runs a pawn shop and other businesses that have nothing to do with fruit.

As if reading my mind, he says, "I give them out in gift baskets with chocolate for Thanksgiving to my customers."

Eleanor and Mike nod.

"That makes sense," I say. "So, you're off the hook. What do you think, Mr. Frackus?"

"I agree with your assessment."

Maddie scribbles in a lined notebook. She grins and shows me a drawing of an old house that looks like the café. In her version, the structure is tilting to the side and on the verge of collapsing. Until this moment, that's how I felt about my inherited mission to run this place. I was about to fall over and seriously unsound with rot at my core. But today, I feel different. After this meeting, I'll move on and take care of business in an upbeat, professional manner. I'll be the Karina I was in the Seattle art studio, when I threw fifty bowls in one day. Another potter looked over and remarked, "She's on fire today!" That will be me.

I wiggle my fingers at Maddie.

"Moving on," I say, "you all know Ellie Robinson and her daughter Maddie. They were here at the time the diary went missing. But they swore they had nothing to do with it."

"It was red," Maddie says. "It was pretty, and I wanted it." She points at Bernard Frackus. "He has it. I saw him with part of it. He was holding a piece of paper with writing on it."

"Hold on there, miss," Bernard says. "That's quite an accusation."

Everyone in the room nods. Mr. Frackus is well-liked

in town. Accusing my teacher is like pointing the finger at the mayor for murder in the church belltower.

Before my imagination runs wild, I say, "Bernard Frackus is a suspect because, as Maddie mentioned, he picked up a page from Gigi's diary in front of the café on Friday."

He waves his hands in the air. "I'm not sure how the page got there. The handwriting caught my eye, so I picked it up. Because I was going out with Gigi for years, I know her handwriting. It is beautiful." He wipes his damp eyes.

A murmur runs through the room.

Eleanor says to Mike, "I didn't know they were going out. Did you?"

Mike shakes his head.

Bill Rafferty and Flash nod to each other, as if they already knew.

"So, we know," I say, "that Bernard Frackus happened to be in the area. But he didn't come into the café that day, so he couldn't have taken it."

Ellie Robinson raises a hand. "Are you sure? I thought I saw him walk out the door and go down the steps when you were busy. Maybe he took it because of his friendship with Gigi, as something to remember her by. Not to make an accusation or anything. I'm just floating an idea for discussion."

Heads turn to Bernard, who frowns.

Boots Brinker tugs on a strand of her long black hair.

"That wasn't Mr. Frackus you saw walking out. It was my dad. We bumped into Mr. Frackus on the sidewalk."

Voices murmur.

Mr. Brinker nods. "I didn't see him in the café. Just out by the sidewalk."

"Thank you," Bernard Frackus says. "I appreciate your support. And I don't like being accused of something I didn't do. All I did was love someone who is gone." He blinks back tears and wipes his eyes.

I put a hand to my heart. My stalwart sidekick, Bernard Frackus, looks torn up. He misses my grandmother. Maybe sitting here talking about her is bringing back tender memories that are too fresh for him. I know how that is. I swallow, feeling grateful that she was loved by so many people.

Wanda speaks up. "I also believe Mr. Frackus didn't come in that afternoon."

I nod. That's settled then.

Wanda says, "I was invited to join this group, so I must be a suspect. And sure, I'm writing a novel about a missing diary. But I don't need Gigi's journal to get my ideas. They come to me as I write. Using someone's actual journal for ideas would cramp my creativity."

She has a point. She looks innocent, and her face is relaxed. But I recall she's an actor and would know how to cover her tracks. I'm wavering and not sure if she's in the clear.

I say, "We'll hold off making judgements or letting

people off the hook at this point. As an actor, I bet you know how to avoid looking guilty."

"That's right," Guns Brinker says. He's wearing purple eyeliner with a black shirt and jeans.

"Thanks, Guns," I say, "I asked you to join us because you were here that fateful afternoon. And I believe you had a motive."

His mouth drops open.

"I've heard you have a certain habit you need money to support?"

He glares at his sister, who told me about his online addiction.

Flash and Bill Rafferty raise their eyebrows.

Mr. Brinker snaps his head, staring at his son. He says, "You'd better have a solid basis for what you're about to say."

"Guns, why don't you tell your dad? It might be better coming from you."

He rakes a hand through his hair. "I've been playing poker online. I was getting pretty good, but then I started losing. I lost a lot."

His dad claps him on the back. "We'll talk about this later. No wonder you asked for your birthday money early." He glances at his phone and says to me, "Let's move on. I've got an appointment."

"Mr. Brinker, I asked you here because you were interested in the diary."

He shrugs. "What of it? It looked interesting is all."

Boots says, "Dad didn't take it. I was the last to leave the table. He walked out first, after paying."

"Understood," I say. "Moving on, Mr. Robinson, you voiced a strong interest in reading the journal because you're interested in history."

Kenny Robinson tugs on the collar of his polo shirt. "Is being curious a crime? If it is, then lock me up." He extends his wrists, as if waiting to be handcuffed.

We all chuckle, in part to release the building tension.

I move on to other suspects. "Shane, Lydia, and Aunt Jean, thank you for joining us."

They nod. Lydia slouches in her seat. Her mom sits ramrod straight like she is on trial. Shane smiles at me.

"Shane, I heard you were in the dining room after the diary went missing. You did say you were interested in learning about Black Monday."

He shrugs.

"Lydia, I know you weren't here because you took off right when I needed you most, and the café was hopping."

"I had to see Shane," she says. "It couldn't wait. We'd had a fight, and I wanted to apologize."

I frown. Nothing is more important than your partner. I get it, but I needed her here working during the crunch time.

"By the way," Lydia says, "I got a new job after school and on Saturdays, so you'll have to hire someone else."

I bite my tongue, suppressing a brutal stream of swear words that flash through my mind. Thanks a lot, Lydia.

Great way to spring the news, right in front of customers. But no problem. I can take it. I'll find someone to replace her who will work steady hours without flitting off when we're busy.

"Good to know," I say. "And congratulations. When is your last day here?"

"Already had it. I'm starting tomorrow working for Mr. Brinker." She flashes a broad smile across the café. "Thanks, Mr. Brinker."

He says, "I didn't know you had obligations here. I don't want to create hardship for Karina." He glances at me with a dash of pity. "This cafe is a lot for one person to run all by herself."

I shrug. "My grandmother did it, and she lived a long, happy life."

Lydia says, "Actually, Karina, I should probably also tell you that I've been working for Mr. Brinker on a trial basis after school and on Saturdays for just a few hours. I was trying it out. That's why I haven't been around much, but you assumed I was goofing off and not showing up. I didn't want to tell you, because I knew you'd be upset. But I have to follow what's best for me, not for you and Gigi."

"Okay," I say, crossing my arms and feeling betrayed at her sneaking around. It seems everyone is keeping secrets behind my back these days, leaving me in the dark. "I guess I'm glad you told me that. We'll talk about it later. But now it looks like I need to hire a part-time helper."

Shane raises his hand. "I'll fill in for Lydia until you find someone else."

Tilting my head, I say, "Really? Are you sure?"

He grins. "I'd be happy to help." He says to the others, "Karina and I went out in high school, so it'll be like old times, hanging out together."

I nod. Even though this is temporary, it'll be fun to laugh and work side by side. "It's a deal. I look forward to it."

Lydia furrows her brow and gives Shane the side-eye.

"And when Shane isn't available," Bernard Frackus says, "I'll fill in."

"Thanks," I say with a wide smile. "That's great. Then I'm all set for staff, for the time being, that is."

I turn to my cousin. "Lydia, I know you weren't here when the diary was discovered. But are you sure you didn't come in for a moment and take the diary? And keep it as something to remember our grandmother by?"

She rolls her eyes. "I wasn't here. I didn't take it. Enough said."

Mr. Brinker raises his eyebrows. She's his problem now, as his newest employee.

My phone rings, and I answer it, putting it on speaker. I've been expecting the call, and I want the group to hear it.

Holding up an index finger as a signal to wait, I say, "Hello?"

"Hi, Jeff and Ned here, calling from Seattle. We didn't have time to drive up on short notice."

"Thanks for calling in. We're partway through the meeting."

Brinker taps his wrist, reminding me of the time.

"We've got to wrap this up," I say. "I appreciate everyone taking the time. And I know you've got better things to do. Ned and Jeff, would you like to introduce yourselves and explain why you're interested in the journal?"

"Sure, I'm Ned, and I'm a reporter. I was working on a story about the journal, but then I was reassigned by my editor to something else. That's why I'm calling in late."

"I'm Jeff, and Karina and I used to go out. Before she broke it off with me."

Shane meets my eyes, raises his eyebrows, and glances away.

Jeff says, "I heard about the diary down here in Seattle and thought it would be cool to own it or at least find it. I heard it contained a treasure hunt with clues."

Eleanor whispers, "Maybe he's got it."

I clear my throat. "Neither of you were in town when the notebook was taken, so you're off the hook. I don't believe either of you took it."

"That's right," Jeff and Ned say in unison.

"Given what we've heard," I say, looking around the café, "who is most likely to have taken it?"

A few people say, "Boots."

Boots says, "Wanda."

Wanda scowls, and it's not a good look on her. "Guns. Maybe. That's my best guess, since he needs money."

Ned over the phone says, "Why Boots and Wanda?"

The cafe quiets down.

"Boots wants to use the journal," I say, "to write a paper for college on the stock market crash on Black Monday and the impact on human behavior. Wanda asked about the journal on her way to the bathroom that day. It could serve as background material for a novel she's writing."

Boots flips her hair back.

Wanda shrugs.

Guilty as charged.

Bernard Frackus clears his throat. "And there's Kenny Robinson. I'm sorry, Kenny, but you could've easily have taken it to add it to your collection of personal histories. Or to give to your daughter."

"No way," Kenny Robinson says. "You know I'm an honest man. I've always given you fifteen percent off on your sneakers as a teacher discount. And I don't do that for everyone."

Bernard Frackus scratches his jaw. "You're right. I'm sorry I mentioned your name. And I appreciate the special treatment."

Eleanor and Mike say to each other, "We've never gotten a discount at his store."

"Settle down," Kenny Robinson says. "Anyone who is

here today can come in and mention the discount. We'll call it Gigi's secret fifteen percent off. But don't tell anyone else. I have to make a profit to stay in business and feed the family."

His wife, Ellie, frowns and taps her fingers on the table.

Kenny glances over at her and quickly says, "Of course, I'm not the only bread winner in the family. Thank goodness, Ellie here has her own thriving law practice."

Ellie brightens and smiles.

Mike says, "Good on ya. I appreciate the discount."

"Thanks, Kenny," Eleanor says, and others chime in. "Thanks."

Mr. Rasmus, the librarian, clears his throat. He's been sitting in the back. "No one has mentioned me."

He's so quiet and unassuming, I'd almost forgotten he was there.

"Who is speaking?" Ned says over the phone.

Mike speaks up. "Our librarian, Mr. Rasmus."

32

Mr. Rasmus stands. The crowd in the café quiets. As far as I know, any one of these suspects could have taken the notebook. I called the meeting, but we're no closer to knowing the truth.

"I'd like to take a moment to say how pleased I am," the librarian says, "to be included in this gathering. As someone who values historic documents, I sympathize with how Karina must be feeling. A loss as great as her grandmother's death has affected all of us in town, and we miss Gigi's positive presence. Especially at the library, where she was a frequent patron. And by frequent, I mean she'd stop in and browse the shelves at least once a week, if not more."

Brinker says, "I'm sorry to interrupt, but can we wrap

this up? I don't want to be rude, but I've got somewhere I have to be."

Boots leans over. "Dad, let the man speak. Don't interrupt him. You'll still make your meeting. This is important."

Right on, Boots. Way to speak up. This is a priority.

Mr. Rasmus's speech reminds me of how much I miss my grandmother. Her laugh rang out like a bell in the café, chiming in the thin-walled house.

I say, "Thank you so much, Mr. Rasmus, for your kind words. You voiced an interest in reading the document, and that's why I asked you here. But I think your name should be struck from the list of suspects, because you weren't here at the time."

He sits down. "Understood. But I appreciated the opportunity to speak. And I hope if you have more meetings like this, you'll include me."

What a sweet man. I say, "Of course, we will, right Mr. Frackus?"

"That's right. We definitely will."

"Include me too," others say. "We want to find out what happens."

Brinker is on his phone texting, perhaps canceling the meeting he mentioned.

Looking around the café, I say, "Thank you all for coming. I have a better idea of people's motives and who was here at the critical time when the diary was taken. But it remains a mystery to me who stole it. Maybe with more time, it'll turn up, and the guilty party will leave it on the café front counter. I guarantee if you do that, there'll be no questions asked. Just drop it and go. Or hand it to me and get a week's worth of free scones and coffee."

Eleanor looks at her notes. "One person hasn't spoken yet."

Silence fills the room, and we crane our necks, looking around.

"Who hasn't spoken?" I say.

My eyes grow wide when my Aunt Jean stands. Her face turns red, and she pulls a red leather diary from her big black purse. "Here it is, Karina. I sorry to say I found it among Lydia's things in her room."

Lydia's eyes open wide, and she claps a hand over her mouth. "Please, not here, not in front of everyone."

My aunt hands me the journal. The red leather cover is soft in my hands.

I hug my aunt and say, "Thank you. I'm so relieved to have it back."

Lydia jumps out of her seat. Before I can stop her, she grabs the notebook from my hand, tucks it into her messenger bag, and runs for the door.

"What's going on?" Ned the reporter says over the phone. "Who has it?"

Bernard speaks into my phone. "It looks like Lydia had it all along. But she's trying to take it back."

Flash quickly moves to block the front exit.

Lydia turns and races toward the back door, but Shane stands in the hallway.

Her bag falls to the floor, and she breaks down in tears. She looks at me and wails. "I wanted something of Gigi's. I loved her and miss her so much. You got the café, but I got nothing."

I wrap my arms around my sobbing cousin.

Weeping in my arms, she says, "I miss her."

"I do too," I say, tears streaming down my face. "Believe me, I wish she was here. But know that you're always welcome in this house to share the memories of our grandmother."

The sound of the coffee bean grinder makes us stop and listen.

Bernard Frackus comes out of the kitchen.

"Your aunt and I think it would be great if everyone hung around and had coffee on the house. We'll bake some scones to celebrate the return of the journal. Make yourselves at home, right Karina?"

"Right," I say, wiping my eyes. "Make yourselves at home."

"I wish I was there," Ned says over the phone.

"Me too," Jeff says from Seattle. "Nothing better than free scones and coffee."

"And a discount on sneakers from Kenny Robinson's store," Mr. Rasmus says.

"Along with a dose of small-town camaraderie," Flash says, flashing a grin.

Mr. Rafferty nods and sits back, surveying the scene.

Bernard brings out a pot of coffee and fills cups.

I'm jittery from all the excitement, so I skip drinking coffee and sit cradling the journal in my hands. A wave of relief washes over me, and I let out a sigh. Although it's small, the book seems heavy, with many possible secrets hidden inside.

Aunt Jean hands out warm scones. She stops to say to me, "My mom meant for you to have the journal. It's clear from her notes in the margins where she mentions your name. I'm so sorry Lydia felt the need to take it."

I smooth my hand over the leather cover. "I understand why she did it, and I'm just glad to have it back."

The others are laughing. Bill Rafferty claps Kenny Robinson on the back about the shoe discount and talks about putting a business deal together. I swear, Bill Rafferty always has something going on.

I find a seat in a corner and open the journal to read my grandmother's entry from Monday, October 19, 1987: "I'll leave a clue for Karina to find the money one day, when she's old enough to use it wisely."

Letting out a low whistle, I make a vow to find it. I want to pay off my student loans and, if there's enough left over, install a second dishwasher, buy a new refrigerator, and buy an electric kiln to fire my pottery.

Time passes as I turn the pages. I'm lost in the book, soaking up details about Gigi's first date with my grandfather, when someone taps me on the shoulder.

"We're going to head out," my aunt says.

I give her a hug and thank her for returning the journal. I say, "I'll be glad to let you read it, after I'm finished with it."

"I already read some of it, after I found it in Lydia's room. Take as long as you like. By the way, I didn't mention I had it with me earlier during the meeting because I was curious how it would go and what everyone would say. I guess I wanted to watch a real-life episode of *Death in Paradise* up close and in person."

Lydia wraps her arms around me, and she smells like sunshine. She says in my ear, "I'm so sorry. I just had to have something of Gigi's."

Pulling her close, I say, "I understand. But you caused me a lot of anxiety and trouble. I hope the embarrassment you're feeling now is enough to stop you from doing other stupid things like this. You've got a new job and a bright future. Take care and don't screw it up."

She steps back and nods. "I won't."

One by one, people trickle out the door as I wave goodbye.

The sound of water running comes from the kitchen, where pots and pans clang. I stop on my way to help whoever is kind enough to be doing the dishes and open a hall closet. I tuck the journal on a shelf. I have a lot more to read before I close my eyes and sleep tonight. Could the notebook possibly hold clues to the identity of my sister? I hope so.

Bernard turns off the tap at the kitchen sink and smiles at me.

Flash sets down a baking pan and hangs the dish towel over the faucet.

I say, "Thanks, guys, I appreciate the help."

Flash grins. "I thought I'd put in some work in return for these scones." He gestures to a white bag on the table. "Your aunt packed some for me to take home. See you later."

He picks up the bag and heads out the back door. For a big man, he sure moves fast.

Bernard says, "Do you need help solving the mystery of the missing money?"

I pat his shoulder. "Go on home. I may need your help tomorrow if I get stuck."

"I'd be glad to help. You can count on it, rain, or shine. It'd be my pleasure to assist you."

I give my old high school teacher a quick hug. I'm happy to consider my grandmother's boyfriend as a family friend. My fingertips tingle, and I can't wait to go upstairs to read the journal. "I'll let you know if I run into a problem."

He says, "Follow the facts. Write down potential clues as you read the journal. Keep them in one place."

I nod and let him out the back door. "I'll do that."

"Don't forget to let me know if you need help," he calls, going to his car.

"I will. Goodnight."

"Night."

All is quiet in the house as I lock the doors. For once, the silence isn't unsettling. Instead, it feels inviting, like it's time to settle down and read a good story on my own.

I pull the red leather covered journal off the closet shelf and hold it in my hand. As I make my way upstairs, I say, "I'm ready to learn your secrets."

I pause at the top of the steps, gripping the handrail, and glance at the closed door to Gigi's room. I realize I'm more interested in learning about my grandmother than in tracking down clues to the money. If I never find the hidden cash, I'll be fine.

33

I open the door and go into my grandmother's bedroom. Settling in her wing chair, I rest my feet on a brown ottoman and throw a blanket over my legs. A tasseled lamp shade on a brass standing lamp looks over my shoulder. It's fitting to be surrounded by her things while browsing through the pages of her personal musings.

I open the journal and smile, reading about how my grandfather proposed while they were out fishing on his boat. He waited until after they'd filleted the two salmon they'd caught, and the fish were on the ice in a cooler.

When he bent down on one knee, Gigi protested.

"Oh no," she'd said. "You're not proposing to me now, covered in fish guts!"

But he did, and she said yes. They were married by a

justice of the peace, with two close friends coming along as witnesses. Gigi was radiant in a sea foam green dress.

I set down the journal. Why haven't I heard this story before? Holding a pen and a lined notebook left over from my college days, I'm ready to scribble down notes. Fishing, proposal, Grandad's boat, green wedding dress, and justice of the peace. Could these be possible clues?

Reading ahead, I learn the wedding reception was held at her parents' house. Of all places, they'd held it in the daylight basement. That's strange. Why not in the living room?

Gigi's handwriting changes in the following pages. The pencil lines are dark, thick, and jagged as if she was distraught. Some words are smudged. I sigh when I learn that after the wedding toasts, my great-grandmother marched over to the two-tiered lemon poppyseed wedding cake and tipped the table over. The cake landed with a splat all over the floor.

My great-grandmother yelled after ruining the cake, "This isn't the wedding I wanted." She stomped out of the room and drove away.

A tear trickles down my cheek, and I wipe my eyes with my bathrobe sleeve. How did Gigi feel after being betrayed like that and embarrassed on her wedding day? With a shudder, I understand why Gigi didn't want to talk about her parents.

Reading ahead, I gasp.

"When my mother made a scene and smashed our

wedding cake, I ran out of the room sobbing. Richard followed me. We got in the car and left for our honeymoon at Lake Crescent Lodge. I was three months pregnant. I haven't spoken to my mother since."

I now realize why she warned me off having sex when I was in high school. I was mortified when we had 'the talk,' but she was trying to protect me. She sat me down twice and shook her finger, as if scolding me. Given the notebook's nuggets of her personal history, it all makes sense.

I wish I'd met my grandfather Rich, but he passed away before I was born. A boating accident took his life too soon. Gigi loved him until the day she died, so she told me.

I open the journal at random to a spot farther ahead and tap my finger on a page. The writing is blurred, as if her tears in the past made the page damp.

"Then I knew what I had to do. I had to keep Karina safe, but I could only do that by conspiring with Bill Rafferty and making him promise to watch over us. I met with Bill, and he said the unsavory characters who caused Karina's parents' deaths would never darken our door. Our little girl would be safe. But I had to make a promise in return."

My pulse quickens. Was Gigi right about how my parents died and the brake lines were cut? Or was Bill Rafferty merely calming her irrational, unfounded worries? I turn the page, but where the next passage should be, there's a ragged edge along the spine of the journal. The page has been ripped out, and it isn't the one Bernard found, so I'm stuck without answers.

I put down the book. "What did you promise? And why promise something to Bill Rafferty? Why is there a page missing?"

I sit back to review what I've learned. Bill Rafferty protects me, supposedly, if her writing in the diary is to be believed. What was the promise Gigi made to Rafferty? Could Rafferty be my real grandfather? Will I ever know the truth?

A headache throbs, and I massage my temples while puzzling over the pieces. The wedding was a fiasco. She was three months pregnant with my mom. Gigi was bitter about her mother's behavior, as anyone in their right mind would be.

I read on, hunched over the journal late into the night, driven by endless questions. What was Gigi's promise in return for my protection? I can't find any answers.

Finally, I turn back to the Black Monday pages in the journal. On the second page of this section, in the margins, I'm startled to read, "I hid a clue in the laundry chute."

The laundry chute? How could she hide something in the laundry chute? I've just thrown clothes down there. I've never examined it.

My pulse quickens. Is this the moment I have been waiting for? A clue?

My hand trembles. I drop the pen on the floor, bound out of the chair, and hurry down the stairs.

Flipping on the basement lights, I hurry down the steps to the basement and past the potter's wheel. The laundry room is located next to the lower-level bathroom.

My heart thumps. The laundry chute ends with a wooden cage next to the washing machine. When I was young, I thought it looked like a jail cell for children. That's why I was scared to come down here. The wooden slats are painted yellow, with two-inch gaps between them.

I crane my neck, looking up the chute. I feel around the opening. Nothing is hidden there. But what about the plywood base?

When I knock on the base, it sounds hollow. Could there be a false bottom with a hidden cavity below? I try to lift the base, but it doesn't budge.

I go over to my grandfather's work bench, which is in the room with the well. Opening a drawer, I pull out a flat-bladed wood-handled screwdriver, an awl, a hammer, and a chisel. It's best to be prepared.

I return to the laundry room and pry at the wood platform, where dirty clothes land before being reborn. Tapping the hammer on the chisel, the metal blade slides in below the base. When I pry, wood splinters. Nails groan and give way. I pull up the plywood and peer underneath.

Goosebumps prick my flesh. In the space are stacks of fifty-dollar bills banded together and a black bank account register. A chill runs up my spine, and I rub my arms.

The money is real. It's right in front of me. The story in the diary wasn't make believe.

"Thank you, Gigi," I whisper, slipping the bank account register into my pocket to open later.

I'm stunned, staring at so much money in one place. And it is in my home. I wonder why she didn't put it back in the bank.

Reaching out, I touch the bills and decide to leave the cash where it is for the time being. I'll figure out a better place to store the money later. I might rent a safe deposit box at the bank to store it.

But I already have plans to spend it. Hopefully, this amount of money will be enough for those plans. To say I am surprised and happy is an understatement.

I raise my arms and do a happy dance, shaking my hips.

"I'm in the money. No worries anymore. Shut the door."

I put my hands on the washing machine and do leg kicks to celebrate.

When I stop a few minutes later, I'm panting and out of breath. With the back of my hand, I wipe my brow.

I lower the piece of plywood over the money and tap it into place with the hammer. When I step back, nothing seems amiss. I go upstairs to study the bank account register.

I whistle as I make a cup of cocoa. Sitting at the table, my knees are jumping up and down with excitement. I open the college notebook where I made notes while reading Gigi's journal and write at the bottom of the page, "Mystery solved."

I set down the pen. My hands are moist as I open the bank account register I took from the secret hiding place. My jaw drops. There is enough in the savings account to pay off my student loans.

I'll go to the bank first thing tomorrow to transfer the money. No wonder Gigi's attorney has been trying to get a hold of me, but I've been too busy to meet with him.

Sitting back with a sigh, I realize that running the café is what I was born to do. It isn't a burden or an obligation to fulfill. I want this life, here and now, in this moment.

What's more, being an artist will mesh well with my owning a café. I'll display art on the walls and in display cases. I'll be an entrepreneur in my hometown, carrying on the family business and creating art.

I think about calling Wanda, my new art writing friend, to share my insights, but I shake my head. The person I want to speak with is my grandmother's boyfriend. He must be wondering how things are going over here.

Taking a chance, I call Bernard even though it's late. "I have something to tell you, but is it too late to call?"

"It's fine. I'm up. I haven't been sleeping well lately with all the excitement."

"I know what you mean, and I wanted you to be the first to know. I solved the puzzle. Thank you for helping me. The mystery wouldn't have been solved without you."

He clears his throat. "No problem, Kit Kat. I was glad to help you."

I cough and swallow tears, reminded of my grandmother's nickname for me.

"Gigi would be happy," I say. "We're quite the team, aren't we?"

"We're unstoppable."

A smile spreads across my face. I'm home, where I was always meant to be.

I say, "We are."

"Sleep well. I'll stop by tomorrow to check on you."

"Good night, Bernard."

"Night."

I glance at the clock. Do I have the nerve to text Violet and ask her to meet for a beer? I nod. I definitely do.

"Sorry to bug you if it's too late," I text. "But do you want to stop over now? I have something to ask you."

Within seconds, Violet responds. "I'll be there in five."

While I wait, I take a few minutes to page through the diary, checking for comments about my unknown sibling. I want to be sure I didn't miss anything. Shaking my head, I set it down. Gigi must have meant to tell me in person, but she didn't get around to it. Or, it could be make-believe and not grounded in reality. In the months before she passed away, pain clouded her thinking.

Violet knocks on the door, and I let her in. She looks deep into my eyes, and I feel oddly calm, as if I'm meeting someone I have known for many years.

I gesture to the back quarters and guide her into the living room with the floral print sofas. "What will it be? Beer or whiskey?"

She eyes me and says, "If we're about to talk about what I think we are, I need a whiskey, and three fingers' worth."

I set the glasses down and sink down beside her on the couch.

"I don't know how to put this," I say, "but are you my secret sister?"

She tosses back a quick swallow and cradles the glass in her hands. "I am, and it is a relief to hear you ask me this. I would've talked to you about it before, but I didn't think you knew, and I wasn't sure how to bring it up."

I turn and face her. "I just found out this week that I had a sibling, but I wasn't sure who it was. How did you find out?"

Violet says, "When I was a kid, I opened a trunk in the attic and found a letter."

For some strange reason, I have a hunch my mother birthed a secret baby. My dad wouldn't have cheated on my mom or had another family. I say, "But why did our mother give birth to me but give you up for adoption? I don't understand that.'

Her eyebrows arch. "I think you have the wrong idea. We don't share a mother."

I cock my head. How can that be? I snap my fingers when it hits me. "Are you saying we were both adopted?"

She shakes her head slowly. "No, Karina, we have the same father. But I didn't want to spring it on you and surprise you out of the blue."

My hands clench. I raise my voice and say, "That's not possible. He was a good man."

Violet says, "Our father was not a saint. He deserted my step mother and me, and we had no idea where he was. All these years, I expected him to come back. And every year on my birthday, I waited for his call. My dad must have come here and married your mother."

I massage my aching jaw. This is opposite what I had assumed happened. It crosses my mind that if my dad had babies with two women, there might be others. "Are there more secret siblings?"

She ruffles her short hair and shrugs. "Who knows. I'm happy for you that you had a good life with him. I wish I could say the same. Have you seen him?"

I tilt my head, confused. "Who do you mean?"

She stares at me. "Our dad."

I reach out and take her hand. "I don't know how to say this, but he died years ago. In a car crash."

She covers her mouth and is silent. Tears run down her cheeks. "Deep in my heart, I guess I'm just a little kid, waiting for him to find me. I wanted him to show up and surprise me. Are you sure he's dead?"

I wince, wishing I wasn't delivering this horrible news. She looks so vulnerable, and not like her usual assertive, energetic self. "I'm sorry, but he's gone."

She puts her hands over her face and blubbers.

I let her be because I know what being bereft is like. She needs to feel what she's feeling with no one bothering her for a bit.

A few minutes later, she sniffs and wipes her eyes. "I thought he didn't care about me. I don't think my step mother even knows he's gone."

"You mean you and your mom never heard he passed away?"

She shakes her head. "We just thought he moved away. What you said answers so many questions."

I say, "He must have wanted to start a new life pretty badly, to have disappeared like that. My mom was driving that night. The roads were icy, and a cat crossed in front of the car."

Violet nods, taking this in.

I bite my lower lip and decide not to tell her about Bill Rafferty protecting me and the possibility of the brake lines being cut, causing my parents' car crash. I'm not sure it is true or that it matters. Looking into it won't bring them back. I've learned a lot in the last few days, and the details are swirling around in my brain.

She says, "My step mom and I assumed he'd contact

us when he was when he was settled. But he didn't. And she didn't bother to track him down. She's feisty and independent. She wasn't going to chase down a man who didn't want her. I never looked for him. I had my own life and too much going on to put energy into finding my dead-beat dad."

"That's rough," I say. "I'm sorry you grew up that way."

Violet shrugs. "It made me tough and taught me to rely on myself."

I break down into tears and sob. "I can't believe it. This is so hard to hear. My father wasn't the man I thought he was."

Tears trickle down Violet's cheeks. I grab a wad of tissues from a box and hand Violet some. Blowing our noses, we make the same honking sound. We look at each other and smile.

I suck in air. I can't believe my dad was a thoughtless jerk and jackass. He abandoned Violet and her mom and started over. What a selfish thing to do.

Violet wipes her eyes. "He was in the military when he lived with us. Did he stay in the service?"

Shaking my head, I say, "No, and he never mentioned it. He didn't like to talk about his past. He said it would only bring up hurt, and no need to dwell on that."

She shrugs. "I guess he moved on and didn't look back. Unbelievable, isn't it?"

"It is."

I scrutinize her features. She has my nose and the

same mouth. Without a genetic test, I'm sure that we are sisters. Our fates are intertwined.

In a quaking voice, I say, "I guess one good thing came out of this. At least we found each other." I reach over and give her a hug. "I've always wanted a sister, and now I have one."

She hugs me back, enveloping me in a tight embrace. "I feel the same."

Her arms feel strong. I let out a ragged sigh. This is a lot to take in all at once. I sift through the many recent realizations swimming through my mind. I have a sister, and she is sitting right here beside me. My dad left a different family behind. He wasn't the man I thought he was. My grandmother left me money, and now I can pay off my student loans, and buy a pottery kiln and kitchen appliances. She set me up to start over as a café owner and an artist in my hometown. Maybe she did know what was best for me after all.

I pull away and blow out a breath. "This is crazy, what you said about our dad. My head is spinning. It'll take me weeks, maybe months or years, to absorb the news."

She nods. "I wasn't sure how to approach you. I'm glad you asked me to come over."

I unfurl my clenched fists, and a wave of acceptance washes over me. I raise my whiskey glass to make a toast. "Here's to my secret sister."

She smiles. "To my new sibling."

A stray thought crosses my mind. I could make jam,

using my grandmother's recipe, with my newfound sister one day. That would be more fun than trying to do it alone.

A grin spreads across my face, and I say, "We're together at last."

Thank you for reading this! If you enjoyed *Secrets at the Café*, please let other readers know what to expect by posting reviews on Goodreads, Amazon and Bookbub.

Interested in Violet's story? Read *The Mother's Threat*!

My next mystery-psychological thriller is Under Jackson Bridge, the first book in a new series.
A small town. A close-knit group of friends. A missing ex-husband who left behind clues to a secret life. She must unravel the puzzle and protect her daughter from heartbreak.

Sign up at www.susanspechtoram.com to be the first to hear about my other books. We'll never share your email and you can unsubscribe at any time.

Follow me on BookBub for updates

ABOUT THE AUTHOR

Susan is writing mysteries, thrillers, and suspense novels. She has worked in corporate communications for biotechnology companies and as an artist. Her essays were published in Mothering Magazine, Twins Magazine and Utne Reader.

Susan grew up near Detroit, Michigan and received a BFA with Honors from University of Oregon and a MBA in Marketing from Seattle University. She lives in a windy part of the Pacific Northwest with her husband and their rescue dog.

[f]

BOOKS BY SUSAN SPECHT ORAM

Shore Lodge

The Thieves

Cabin Eight

The Mother's Threat

Secrets at the Café

Under Jackson Bridge

Missing Man

By Midnight

Humorous fiction:

Boating with Buddy, a report from a canine correspondent

Nonfiction:

Brief business books on investor relations, crisis
communication and public relations are available on
Amazon.com.

Made in United States
Orlando, FL
10 December 2024

55330929R00163